Coble's Flash Fiction Volume I

By A.R. Coble

Contents

The Genie 6

The Knife 9

The Teacup 14

Anytos the Demigod 17

Hide and Seek 21

The Wishing Well 24

The System 28

Creature of Habit 31

Personal Demons 34

The Loyalty of a Friend 37

Living in Her Shadow 40

Zombie Sacrifice 43

Fallen Soldier 46

A Husband's Dream 49

A Dream Come True 52

Teen Parenthood 56

Choices 59

Together 62

Accepting a Werewolf 65

Trick or Treat 68

Nevariel's Inheritance 71

Sarra's Wedding 74

Tobias' Sacrifice 77

The King's Discovery 80

Odin's Prickly Memories 82

Acknowledgments 83

Patsy,
It's such an honor to call you my friend. I hope you enjoy these stories!
Love you!
Andrea Coble

The Genie

The genie told her she'd regret her wishes. Ever since meeting him, Sameera's life had changed. At first it seemed like it had changed for the better when she found Rifat's lamp and he offered to grant her three wishes. You see, Sameera's life was not an easy one. Her family was poor and they were often ridiculed by the others in her town because of it. When Rifat made his offer, she saw a chance for her family to live comfortably and to be accepted by the others in their town.

Her first wish was for wealth. "I don't want to be filthy rich, but I want our family to be able to live comfortably and without fear of going hungry," Sameera wished.

Rifat grinned wickedly. "As you wish," Rifat said.

Before she knew it her home had been transformed. It was bigger, luxurious and, Sameera discovered, they were able to hire a cook to shop for and prepare all of their meals. Sameera was pleased with herself for providing such luxury for her family, even if they didn't know she was the cause.

At dinner that evening her brother, Hamad, had some terrible news to deliver. "Our neighbor lost his seven-year-old son in a tragic accident today," Hamad announced with great sadness.

Sameera was sad for her neighbor. To lose a child is a terrible thing. She wouldn't wish it on anybody.

The next day Sameera went back to Rifat's lamp to make her second wish. "Rifat, I wish for our family to be looked on favorably by the others in our town."

Again, Rifat smiled wickedly as he said, "As you wish."

When Sameera and her family went into town later that day to conduct business everyone was friendly to them. Her family acted like it was the norm, though it wasn't, and Sameera was again very pleased with herself. It warmed her heart to experience acceptance from the people in the town.

As they approached a shop, Sameera noticed that a man was holding the shop owner at knife point. The shop owner was a friend of the family and Sameera feared for his life. The man with the knife stabbed the shop owner multiple times in the chest, took as many items as his arms could carry, and fled.

As others swarmed around the dead shop owner a thought occurred to Sameera. The genie told her she'd regret her wishes. What if each wish meant a sacrifice had to be made elsewhere? Sameera's heart broke at the thought. She decided she would visit Rifat tomorrow and ask him about it before making her third and final wish.

The next day she asked Rifat, "Why did you say I would regret my wishes?"

Rifat smiled wide, realizing that she must have figured out the consequences of her wishes. "I think you know what happens," he said with mirth.

"Someone has to die every time I make a wish, don't they?" Sameera had to know, but feared the truth.

Rifat nodded. "So, my dear. What will your third wish be?"

Sameera couldn't make another wish without knowing more. "What happens if I wish for my previous wishes to be undone, restoring everything, including lives, back to the way things were?"

Rifat shook his head in mock sadness, "I'm afraid the lives that have been lost cannot be restored. You may wish for everything else to be restored, but once somebody is gone, they are gone forever."

Sameera's mind reeled at the news that the lives lost couldn't be restored. How could she be so selfish? If she couldn't restore those lives, what could she possibly wish for that would be worth the life of another?

"I'm not ready to make my final wish, Rifat. I'll be back," Sameera said thoughtfully.

"Take your time, my lovely," he said, rubbing his hands together.

Sameera returned home and went straight to her bedroom. Lying on her new plush mattress, she sobbed for the lives that were lost because of her selfish wishes. The seven-year-old boy. His family had to be hurting so much. The shop owner was one of the only men in town who treated her family with dignity and respect *before* the wishes were granted. She grieved and chided herself all night long for the wishes she'd made.

When dawn came she had come to a resolution. Without eating breakfast, or saying goodbye to her family, she went to the cave where she found Rifat in his lamp. She rubbed the lamp furiously, ready to get her final wish over with.

"Early morning or late night?" Rifat taunted.

"I know what my third wish will be, Rifat," Sameera replied firmly.

Rifat caught on to the anger and fierce energy that was emanating from Sameera. What he didn't catch on to was where that anger was directed, and what it would lead to. "Wish away, my dear. And then, sadly, we shall part ways forever."

Sameera smiled sadly and victoriously, making her third and final wish. "I wish for you and other genies like you to be destroyed, and for the cost of this wish to be my own life."

Rifat's eyes went wide. He did not expect a wish like this. As a genie, he was bound by laws of the universe to fulfill this wish. With great fear and disbelief Rifat replied, "As you wish."

The ground shook like a massive earthquake while dust and rocks swirled around Rifat. Sameera shielded her eyes with her arms as a bright light began to emanate from Rifat's lamp, snaking its way up his body. Soon, the light began to burst from his body as though it were destroying him from within.

Sameera heard what sounded like the screams of a thousand genies dying at the same time. Rifat's lamp fell to the ground and disintegrated, Rifat disappearing in a puff of smoke. Soon after, Sameera felt weak as she collapsed to the ground. Breathing became more difficult. Finally, she passed on in the knowledge that she rid the world of an evil source of magic, but not before giving her family everything she ever wanted for them. The genie was wrong. She didn't regret the wishes. She regretted the consequences.

The Knife

The knife shone wicked in the moonlight. Parker studied the shining blade, contemplating the value of his life. He had found a stump in the wooded area just beyond the park to sit and contemplate a decision he'd been struggling with most of his fifteen years of life.

He didn't feel like he could do it anymore. The world he lived in was hell. There were good things, sure, but the darkness that existed was overwhelming. His parents had been fighting a lot lately. Though they both told him that the fighting had nothing to do with him, he felt like it must be his fault. He wanted to fix what was wrong in their relationship, but he was failing miserably.

School went pretty well for him and he thought about all the friends he had in band. They were like a second family to him and no matter how many times they told him how cool he was, or how great of a friend he was, he could never shake the feeling that there was no way he was good enough to deserve them.

His counselor had told him that these are the types of things that happen when anxiety and depression take over. She told him that he would be able to see the logical side of things. Things like how much his family loved him, how much his friends accepted and needed him. But when the anxiety and depression would rear its ugly head, he would be of two minds: seeing the logical, but believing the illogical.

Parker was so deep in thought he hadn't noticed that somebody had joined him.

"Whatcha got there," the other kid asked.

"It's a knife," Parker replied, staring at the knife like it held the answers to his questions.

"I got that," the kid said. "What do you plan to do with it?"

"I don't have a plan yet," Parker replied solemnly. "That's why I'm here. I'm thinking about making a plan."

"Don't do it," the kid replied. "I know it seems like the best option, but it's not."

Another kid appeared out of nowhere on the other side of Parker. "But it is the best option," the new kid said. "Your parents will stop fighting if you're gone..."

The other kid interrupted, "Your parents assured you that the fighting isn't your fault. They would miss you so much if you followed through with this. And what about your friends? They would miss you too!" The other kid was desperate now, trying to convince Parker to stick around.

"Pfffft," the new kid retorted. "Nobody will *actually* miss you," he said. "Sure, if you die they'll all cry for a while, but then they will just carry on like nothing ever happened. Not only will they forget about you eventually, but they'll be better off without you."

The other kid began to cry. "Parker, you know that what he's saying isn't logical. Please, see reason."

The new kid stood up and marched over to the other kid. "You're weak, and it makes Parker weak. Can't you see he needs this? He needs a way out!"

The other kid stood up to the new kid. "What you're telling him to do is selfish! It will hurt everyone who ever cared about him. Especially those who still do. So many people love Parker!"

The new kid scoffed. "You can't be serious! If his parents loved him, they wouldn't fight. If his friends cared, they'd be here right now instead of us!" He turned to Parker, "Can't you see that this is the answer you've been looking for? Look at that knife and tell me I'm not right. All the pain can end, tonight. For you, your family, and your friends. It's the only thing that makes sense!"

Parker stood up and began pacing, thoughtfully turning the knife over in his hand. He was crying now. He could see both sides, just like his counselor had said. He could see the truth, the logic. The illogical thoughts were taking over. They both had excellent points in Parker's now clouded mind.

The other kid said, "Parker, your counselor made you promise that if you were ever in this situation that you wouldn't do anything without talking to her first."

The new kid scoffed, "Of course she's going to tell you to not go through with it. She's legally obligated!"

"Legally obligated or not, she can help you, Parker. You should call her, or call the hotline number she gave you. It's in your phone," the other kid insisted.

Parker touched the phone that was in his pocket and continued to pace, the knife still shining and twinkling in the moonlight.

"Parker, that knife is your ticket! Take the train to the other side and be done with all of it. No more worrying about your parents, your friends, the darkness that consumes this world. You can leave it all behind!"

Parker shouted at the new kid, "Shut UP!" "I can't think straight, and you're being really aggressive about this." He reached for his phone, dialing the number of the one person that he felt certain could help him make his choice.

Later that evening

Parker's counselor stayed on the phone with him until the police arrived at the park. The other kids were gone for the time being, and the police took him to the hospital for evaluation and to keep him on watch. His parents and counselor met him there.

"I'm so glad you called me, Parker. I know the struggle, and I know how strong and brave you were to make that call," his counselor told him.

"Oh, Parker," his mom said, tears pouring down her eyes in waterfalls. That was all she could say. Instead of using the words she could not find, she held him and must have kissed his head a thousand times.

His father looked wrecked, seated in a chair across the room. Amidst the kisses from his mother, Parker made eye contact with his father. The look he saw in his father's eyes made him completely certain that he'd made the right choice. He couldn't bear the idea that he would have caused his father to permanently be in that kind of pain.

A note from the author:

Dear Reader,

If you are struggling with suicidal thoughts, please know that you are not alone! I see you, and I see your struggle. I get your struggle because I have been there. If you can, participate in counseling or a support group. It doesn't make you weak to participate, it makes you strong. Find the help that's available to you locally, and check out the links and phone numbers below for more immediate help - PUT THEM IN YOUR PHONE!

Resources:

National Suicide Prevention Lifeline 1-800-273-8255

Chat with an online SPL counselor: http:www.suicidepreventionlifeline.org/GetHelp/LifelineChat.aspx

Veterans Crisis Line: 1-800-273-8255 (press 1 during the menu)

Veterans Crisis Online Chat: http://www.veteranscrisisline.net/Chat (Click on the dark red button in the top right labeled "Confidential Veterans Chat")

Text to 838255 (Available 24/7)

There are many more resources available (too many to list here) on the internet. This is how much people care!!

Remember these things:

*I see you

*I see your struggle

*You are not alone

*Nobody is better off without you because your soul is BEAUTIFUL

*There is help, and there are people who care! Really!!

With love and respect,

Andrea

The Teacup

"Georgie, stop playing with that!" His really old aunt shouted at his seven-year-old self. He'd picked up one of her precious teacups. He really couldn't help it. He was just so curious! His aunt left the room as he started to put the teacup down. She expected him to leave it alone even though she wasn't right there?! Georgie shook his head in awe. Grown-ups. They didn't use their thinkers!

As soon as she rounded the corner of the doorway out of the room, Georgie lifted the teacup again, examining it. He tried to figure out why this teacup was so precious to his aunt. It was pretty, as much as Georgie could imagine pretty things are. It just didn't seem to have anything super special about it. Georgie wondered just how angry his aunt would get if he dropped it to the floor, watching it shatter into so many pieces.

Georgie's thoughts were soon interrupted by his little brother, Buck. Buck was different from Georgie because Buck really enjoyed making grown-ups happy. Georgie didn't always understand his little brother, but as long as Buck left his toys alone, he was usually ok having the kid around.

"Georgie, you're not supposed to have that," Buck whisper-yelled.

"I know I ain't supposed to have it, Buck. I'm just studying it, so leave me alone," Georgie whisper-yelled back.

And wouldn't you know, a fight ensued. Buck reached for the teacup, attempting to snatch it out of Georgie's hands. Georgie was fast, like lightning, and soon had it up above his head where Buck couldn't reach it.

Buck whispered, "Georgie, you'd better give me that cup before I go tell our auntie that you're up to no good."

"You go on ahead, Buck," Georgie replied, not caring. "I'll have this cup back in its pretty little spot and I'll be halfway through the field before you and Auntie get back."

This infuriated Buck. Why couldn't Georgie just do the right thing? If Georgie wasn't going to do the right thing, then Buck was just gonna have to make him.

"Give me that teacup, Georgie," Buck whisper-yelled before beginning to climb up Georgie's overalls to get to the cup.

Georgie did not expect this. He knew Buck was always hung up on making the grown-ups happy, but he'd never seen him so mean about it. Buck was behaving like a jungle cat, for cryin' out loud!

Next thing he knew, Buck had grabbed the teacup out of Georgie's hand, but Buck hadn't had a good grip on it. They both scrambled to get to the teacup before it hit the ground, but they just couldn't get a hold on that fine piece of drinkware. The teacup shattered as it hit the ground and Buck immediately had big ol' alligator tears in his eyes.

Auntie came rushing around the corner, her eyes wide in disbelief. "What have you boys done to my teacup?" she shrieked.

"Georgie did it!" Buck wailed.

Georgie looked at his brother, eyes wide. Buck knew darn well that Georgie didn't drop that teacup. Georgie caught on pretty quickly that Buck was scared of ruining his reputation as "the good boy." He was also afraid of their aunt, so Georgie didn't deny it when his brother accused him, and his aunt took Buck at his word.

"George Herbert Swanson! I told you not five minutes ago to leave that cup alone, and now it is shattered beyond repair!" his aunt shrieked. She looked panicked, heartbroken, and angry all at the same time.

Georgie knew that teacup was precious and he wouldn't have smashed it on purpose, but seeing his aunt this way was heartbreaking.

"That teacup belonged to my mother, and her mother, and her mother's mother..." their aunt murmured to nobody in particular.

Georgie said, "Auntie, I'm so, so sorry. I should have left it alone when you told me and I should have listened to Buck when he told me not to mess with it, too." His heart was hurting for his aunt. He was so mesmerized by it that he barely registered that Buck was staring at him in awe. Clearly, he didn't think that Georgie would take the blame.

Their aunt made Georgie clean up every last shard. She stood there and watched him to make sure he did as he was told this time.

"Auntie, can I help him?" Buck asked?

His aunt stared at him for a moment, not altogether shocked that Buck would offer to help. He was the better of the two boys, after all. His aunt shook her head and said, "No, Buck. Not this time. Georgie needs to learn that when grown-ups tell him to leave things alone, it's for a good reason and not just to be uptight fun-killers."

So, Buck watched Georgie clean up every last shard. Georgie didn't complain and did his job quietly. Once it was cleaned up their aunt sent both of the boys outside to play where they couldn't break any other teacups.

"Why'd you do it, Georgie?" Buck asked with intense curiosity.

"I was curious about that cup," Georgie replied. "I wanted to study it to see if I could figure out why it was so important to Auntie."

"No," Buck said, shaking his head. "I mean, why did you take the blame when I'm the one who grabbed it out of your hands and dropped it?" Buck's eyes threatened to tear up.

"Oh, well, that was easy," Georgie said. "I could see how scared you were. I felt bad for you, and for auntie, and I started it all. It was just the right thing to do, you know?"

Buck shook his head in amazement. "You're better than the grown-ups say you are," Buck whispered in astonishment. "If they only knew..."

Georgie interrupted, "Don't go telling people I'm good, Buck! They'll expect it from me all the time!"

Anytos the Demigod

He blinked and she was gone. A hundred years Anytos had waited for his beautiful goddess and just like that, she was snatched away by Hades. The air didn't supply enough oxygen when Persephone wasn't near. His thirst could not be quenched unless she was by his side.

He would rescue his beloved. He would need some help. He was only a demi-god after all, and he was going up against a major god. He approached his best friend, Periphetes, with the plan.

"We'll need to gain the trust and control of Hades' alpha hound," Anytos told him.

"That's no easy task, there, Anytos." Periphetes was skeptical, and rightly so. Nobody had ever taken out a major god before. Killing Hades was the only way for Anytos to win his prize and, goddess or not, he couldn't see how she was worth the cost.

"I understand this, Periphetes," Anytos replied in exasperation. He pleaded with his friend to hear the rest of the plan.

Periphetes listened and only agreed to go along with it because of the desperation in his best friend's eyes.

The next morning the two of them set off to one of the few known entrances into the Underworld. This particular entrance was found in a dark cave where water lurked in the ceiling and dripped on unsuspecting trespassers, burning through their clothing and into their skin to keep them away. This did not deter Anytos and Periphetes. They wore extra layers of leathered gear and carried an ox skin over their heads to protect them from the burning water.

They made their way to the back of the cave where they found the cavern that goes down deeper than even the demi-god eye can see. Right into the Underworld. They tossed their ox skins aside, looking at each other.

Anytos asked, "Are you in this with me, friend?"

Periphetes took another look at the deep, dark hole they intended to jump into to rescue Anytos' lover. If he weren't so loyal, he might have changed his mind. Periphetes looked back at Anytos, grinning at him like he always did when they were about to get into some trouble together and said, "To the end, my friend. To. The. End."

Anytos returned his friend's grin. They leapt into the giant cavern, resisting the urge to scream as they fell for what felt like eternity. Finally, they landed. Anytos landed so hard that it knocked the breath out of him. He was seeing spots for a few minutes while he struggled to catch his breath.

Periphetes, however, was struggling to stay quiet. He had landed on his knees, crushing both of his knee caps.

When Anytos caught his breath, he noticed that Periphetes was in pain. He ran over to his friend and knelt beside him. "Periphetes, what happened?!"

Periphetes gritted his teeth, still trying to keep from screaming. The pain was unbearable. He gritted his teeth, "I. Landed. On. My. Knees," he got the words out slowly and with great effort.

Anytos' eyes went wide.

"You...need...to...go...on...without..."

Anytos didn't let his friend finish that sentence. "I know that you're right, but I can't just leave you here. Let me find a safe place for you. Once I've defeated Hades I'll come back." He didn't like the idea of leaving his best friend there, but what choice did he have?

Periphetes shook his head. "Leave...me. I'll...manage."

Anytos started to argue, but Periphetes gave him a look that he knew well. It meant that Periphetes would not brook any refusal on the matter. Anytos also knew better than to argue with him when he reached that point.

Anytos gave a nod and began his search for the alpha hound. The hounds weren't difficult to find. Their stench was legendary and it led Anytos directly to their kennels. Fortunately, their kennels were labeled with their names and ranks within the pack, but they didn't have doors. They could come and go at any time.

Anytos walked as quietly as possible down the hallway, silently reading the names and ranks of each hound as he passed. He saw one for Agatha. She was pretty low on the totem pole. He saw another for a hound named Pinder. He was the Beta.

Finally! Anytos found the alpha hound, Lois. She was in her kennel fast asleep. Very carefully he pulled out the parcel that contained the very special treats that he brought for Lois. The treats were various parts from the ox they slaughtered to get through the cave. They included the liver, the heart, the stomach, and other organs. The innards were a hound's favorites. Lois woke up quickly when she smelled them.

Anytos and Lois came to a quick understanding. She and the pack would leave him alone. He would confront Hades and when he won, he would bring her similar treats every day for a hundred years.

Anytos turned to exit the kennels to find Hades standing in the large, arched entryway. Beside him Persephone stood, beauty beyond understanding, with the saddest eyes Anytos had ever seen. On Hades' other side, bound in fiery rope, was his best friend. Periphetes hung limply in the air, bound, unconscious.

Hades sneered, "You think you can best me by winning the stomach of my hound?!"

Anytos readied himself for battle, his own fire burning hot in his eyes.

"You'll never have her, you pathetic little demi-god," Hades smirked. "And as for your friend, let's just say he'll be swimming in the River pretty soon," Hades taunted.

Anytos let rage consume him and he attacked the arrogant god. They battled and struggled until, finally, Anytos had Hades pinned to the ground.

"This is for Periphetes!" Anytos punched Hades in his god-face. "And this is for Persephone!" He swung his sword high and beheaded the god of the Underworld.

Persephone cried, "What have you done?!"

Confusion was all that filled Anytos' mind. It was like a fog, swirling, and thick.

"If you kill Hades, you must take his place," Persephone sobbed.

Anytos felt the shift from demi-god to god of the Underworld taking place. Panic arose knowing he could now never be with

Persephone. He would not keep her prisoner in the Underworld and he knew she could not bear to stay.

    Sadness filling his every thought, he walked over to his friend, who now lay on the ground, dying. A new plan formed in his mind. He healed Periphetes and asked Persephone to join them. He made his friend promise to marry her, take care of her, and give her everything she ever wanted.

    Anytos watched as the woman he loved walked away with his best friend. All of them shedding tears for what they lost that day. Anytos sat on his throne in the Underworld weeping for the rest of eternity while Lois drank up his tears.

Hide and Seek

She closed her eyes, then counted to ten. This whole thing started as a game of hide and seek with her little brother, Kato, but when Yagi opened her eyes she was no longer in the Shinjuku Gyoen National Garden. She loved her brother more than anything. He was the only family she had left and she was responsible for him.

It was nearly pitch black, but she could see enough to know the mirrors that now surrounded her reminded her of the latest American horror movie. Her long, straight black hair hung as dark curtains around her face, her image reflected in each of the mirrors as she looked around for Kato. He wasn't there.

"Kato! Kato!" she shouted over and over again. Panic was beginning to well up inside her. She quickly turned it into fuel to begin searching for him. Yagi wouldn't look at the mirrors on the walls. Instead, she would look at the floor. It was a few feet wide, the size of a hallway, and she would just follow the floor out, calling for Kato as she went along.

Every ten feet or so she called out for her brother and received no response. Several times she had reminded herself to keep calm. She couldn't find Kato if she lost her head. About three hundred feet and multiple turns later she heard Kato respond when she called out to him.

"Hold on, Kato! I'm coming for you!" She crawled faster and faster. "Kato, keep talking to me so I can follow your voice!" she instructed him.

Kato wasn't talking, she realized. He was using his voice, but it sounded muffled like he'd been gagged. This put a new fire in Yagi's belly and she crawled even faster towards the sound of Kato's voice when, all of a sudden, she discovered something that was blocking her path.

They were oversized red shoes. She reached out to touch them, hoping they were just a prop for this madhouse. When she pulled her fingers back it left streaks in the red on the shoes. She looked at her fingers and they were red now. She lifted her shaking fingers to her nose and nearly threw up. The shoes were red because they were covered in blood.

Yagi looked back at the shoes, then noticed the crazy pattern on the socks that led her eyes upwards to see the most terrifying clown she had ever laid eyes on. He was looking down at her, smiling maniacally. Painted face and red nose. Rainbow colored afro, teeth that had been filed to sharp points, blood dripping from his mouth.

Yagi screamed as the clown reached out to grab her, but she was small and quick, and had more interest in living than just self-preservation. Her brother's life was at stake and he would not die on her watch. She made a quick dive around the clown, tucking into a ball and landing on her feet on the other side. She kept calling for Kato as she ran, asking him to use his voice to lead her to him.

She found him, but didn't have time to sigh with relief. She had no doubt that the crazy clown was not long behind her. She had little time to rescue her brother and get him out of there before they both died. Kato was tied to a chair and gagged. His right forearm was free, but it was dripping with blood where the psychotic clown had clearly bitten into it.

Yagi freed her brother and asked if he knew how to get out of there. Both of their eyes found the bright red sign that read "EXIT" in English, and they ran hard for the door. Kato was still losing blood and the running made his blood run out faster. He paled quickly and collapsed before the exit, right on top of the skeletons of a man and a woman.

Yagi shook her brother, hoping to snap him out of it, but it didn't work. She slapped his face and that didn't work either. She checked his pulse and it was still there, but weaker than she'd like. Just then, the clown appeared with a hungry and satisfied smile. Yagi understood that he'd caught both of them and, though the exit was just behind them, they wouldn't be able to make it out before he ate them for supper.

Just as the clown reached for Yagi, she woke up. She was in her bed, sweat and tears dampening her sheets. Breathing hard, she allowed herself to catch her breath before getting up. She was relieved that it was just a dream, but she couldn't shake the feeling that it really happened.

She walked into the kitchen, ready to eat some breakfast. Her parents were in there, speaking in hushed tones. The food smelled so good. She felt like she'd run a marathon and could use a big breakfast. Her father was at the stove, an unusually big smile on his face as he prepared breakfast for Yagi and her mother, who was already seated at the counter.

"Yagi, we have big news to share with you," her mother said. She was glowing and she looked beautiful.

Yagi sat down next to her mother as she waited for them to share their big announcement.

"You're going to have a brother!" her mother announced.

Yagi nearly spit out her juice. She'd had a brother in her dream, but until her mother's very recent pregnancy, she was an only child. Something didn't feel right.

"That's wonderful news, Haha," Yagi forced out. "What will his name be?" She had to know. What were the chances?

"His name will be Kato, and you will share in the responsibility of taking care of him," her father said proudly.

Five years later

Yagi's parents had been missing for six months. The responsibility of being her brother's caretaker weighed heavy on her. She had taken Kato for a walk in the Shinjuku Gyoen National Garden. Kato, not noticing in his innocence that Yagi was deep in contemplative thought, asked his sister to play a game of hide and seek. Having forgotten the dream she had five years earlier, she agreed, closed her eyes, and counted to ten.

The Wishing Well

The wishing well was feeling stubborn today. You see, the well had been granting wishes for centuries and it was so very tired of doing so. The well thought that it was high time it got a wish granted of its own. Being a wishing well, it couldn't grant its own wish directly. It would have to convince some poor sap to do it instead. The well spent days scoping out which wisher it would choose.

An old man came by the well to make a wish.

"Before you make a wish, might I make a suggestion?" the well asked.

The old man huffed. "Why would I let you do that?"

The well, cunning and scheming, replied with a question, "What is your profession?"

The old man pinched the lapels of his finely tailored suit between his fingers, bouncing up on his toes. "Why, I'm the local banker. People come to me when they need a loan, or to plan for their future."

"That's fine, indeed," the well replied. "You're a bit of a wish granter yourself, it sounds like."

"Say, I suppose I am," the banker replied. His ego was being well-stroked by the well's flattery.

"Then suppose you grant *me* a wish, Mr. Banker," the well replied.

"What wish would a wishing well have?" asked the banker

"I wish to be free," the well replied simply

The banker laughed. "If I wish you free, then I won't get my wish!" he replied.

The well was displeased, but bound to serve, so he granted the banker's wish.

A mother of ten boys came by. She almost looked exhausted enough for even the well to take pity on her. But nevertheless, the well pressed on.

"Before you make your wish, dear woman, would you consider a suggestion?" the well asked hopefully.

"I'm always being asked to do something or other. I really just want this wish to be mine," the woman said tiredly.

"Oh, I understand completely," the well replied. "Imagine centuries of it! Day in, day out, granting wishes multiple times a day. It's exhausting."

The woman took some pity on the well and decided to hear it out. "What is your suggestion?"

"Wish for my freedom," the well implored her.

The woman thought for a few moments. She couldn't imagine centuries of being pulled in different directions day after day. However, she still couldn't shake her own wish off for someone, no - some*thing* else.

"I'm so sorry, but I just can't do that. I need my wish to be fulfilled." The woman made her wish, and the well granted it. Only because it had too, mind you.

Finally, a little girl came by. She was so very sweet and her hair hung in dark brown braids on either side of her freckled face. Her brown eyes were soft and welcoming.

This is it! The well thought. *This girl is my ticket!* "Before I grant your wish, may I offer a suggestion?" the well asked the little girl.

"Well, I guess so," the little girl replied. "I already know what I came to wish for, though."

"Do you?" the well asked.

The girl nodded emphatically.

"I suppose you wouldn't be interested in hearing what a very old, very wise well would have to say then."

The girl thought a moment. "What's the harm? If I don't like what you have to say, I can still make my own wish, right?"

The well rippled, attempting to conceal its laughter. "Yes, you most certainly can."

Though, the well was certain it could convince her to set him free. The well told her its sad story of how it had been granting wishes for so long. How so many of the wishes were selfish and would cause pain to others. How it couldn't bear to do that any longer.

"What if I used my wish to set you free? What would happen?" the little girl asked sympathetically.

"I would be free, child! I would no longer have to grant wishes and I could see the world!" the well replied. It could almost taste freedom.

The girl pouted her lips in deep thought. "I suppose I could, but what would happen to my wish?"

The well didn't want to answer that. It was afraid of her reaction to the news. "I'm afraid you would have to find a different wishing well, child."

The girl was consumed with emotion for this well. It pulled at just the right heart strings and she could bear it no longer. "Then I wish for your freedom," the girl said with a tear streaming down her face.

Magic swirled around the well in yellow and green sparks. The water swirled up from the well, knocking the little girl backwards onto the soft green grass. She shielded her eyes from the magic light and water. As the water rose higher it formed an arch and deposited a man on the ground, fully clothed.

He looked dazed for a moment, but then he started to study his hands and other limbs. He grabbed his face with both hands in disbelief. The magic died down with the water as it swirled back down into the well. The man ran over to the little girl.

"You sweet, sweet girl," the man exclaimed. He grabbed her gently by the shoulders, a tear in his eye as he whispered a thank you. Finally, he noticed the tear in the little girl's eye.

"What is it?" he asked. "Are you crying for the wish you lost?" he asked gently.

The little girl nodded.

The man, who was once the granter of wishes in the well, sat down in front of her. "What would your wish have been?" He asked his question softly.

"I was going to wish for my brother's life to be saved. He's sick and he's dying. My family doesn't know what to do," the little girl sniffled.

Now in his mortal body, the well realized how selfless this girl had been. Her selflessness gleamed and cast a shadow over his own choice to manipulate this little girl into setting him free.

The System

They don't make handcuffs like they used to. Jexica was unbelievably grateful for it as she rewired the cuffs and slipped right out of them. What was she charged with? Penal code A739 which states: A woman shall not be out of doors without a man present. Punishment is ninety days in holding.

Well, Jex didn't have ninety days to sit around. Her little brother, Duglas, was at home waiting for her to come back. He was probably panicking by now, wondering what happened to her. He was very imaginative too, so he could be thinking anything from *she just got held up* to *oh, my stars, she's dead, isn't she?!* For an eleven-year-old, he was quite the worry wart.

Jex used the disabled cuffs to disable the lock on her door. Fortunately, they put female curfew breakers in a room with a regular door and bars on the window, rather than in the lock-up facility where all walls but one of them are made of bars. Jex shuddered at the thought. She would have had to share a lock-up cell with both men and women if she'd done something to warrant *that* type of punishment.

Making her way down the hall, Jex ran into some guards. They were arguing about something and she utilized their distraction to hide behind a piece of furniture. Jex looked across the hallway and saw a face in the small window of one of the doors. The face belonged to another girl about her age. The girl pleaded with her eyes. She mouthed through the window, "Help me."

One of the guards stormed away toward a different hallway and the other guard followed. Jex released a breath she'd been holding and stood up. There was no way she was going to help this girl. She had to get home to Duggie. She was all he had. Their parents died months ago and now they clung to each other like security blankets.

Jex still had the cuffs, though, and couldn't help but think about the other poor girl who had pleaded with her for help. Jex rolled her eyes at herself. She knew she would regret it, but this girl was the only one asking for help. It's not like she'd have to rescue all of the girls in holding. Looking both ways down the hall, and keeping a wary ear out for the guards, Jex used her cuffs to open the girl's door.

Jex grabbed the girl's hand and put a finger to her lips, willing the girl to be completely silent. She motioned for the girl to stay right behind her and the girl obeyed. Rounding a corner, Jex saw one of the guards' weapons lying on the floor, fully charged. What luck! She picked it up quietly and continued searching for an exit with the other girl following closely behind her, still silent.

Down the hall, around another corner, and Jex saw it. The exit she'd been looking for. They made a run for it and made it through the doors only to be met with guards on the other side. "What are you doing out of your rooms?" one of the guards shouted. "Oy! She has a weapon!" another shouted in alarm.

Jex pointed the gun at the guards, not at all wanting to have to use it. She would, though, if it meant that she could make it home to her brother.

"Put down the gun, miss. Nobody wants to hurt you here," one of the guards said to her with his arms in the air. The other guard had his hand on his weapon, ready to draw if the need arose.

"I just want to go home," Jex said. "If you let me leave in peace, there won't be any trouble."

"You know we can't let you do that, miss," the guard with his hands up replied. "You're in holding because you broke penal code A739..."

"I know why I'm here, sir," Jex replied. "It's archaic that this code even exists. Women are quite capable of protecting themselves."

"Whether it is archaic, right, wrong, what have you...it's still the law, miss. And you broke it," the guard replied.

"You don't understand," Jex said with her teeth gritted and spit flying from her mouth. "I have someone I need to protect and he's home, all alone, and probably scared to death that his only living relative isn't living anymore." Tears threatened her eyes and she became more and more desperate. "Let us pass without incident, or there will *be* an incident."

The second guard with his hand on his weapon began to draw, and Jex didn't think. She just fired the weapon at the man who intended to do the same to her. He fired his weapon at the same time, hitting Jex in the stomach. It took a minute to register the pain from it. In that minute she turned the weapon on the other guard.

"Please don't make me do this again," she said, crying now as the pain was becoming more and more apparent.

The guard kept his hands up and the other girl wrapped Jex's free arm around her neck. She wrapped her arm around Jex's waist, and they walked backwards through the final set of doors. They ran together, the other girl still supporting Jex. They found a hiding spot between a couple of old buildings where the girl set Jex down carefully.

"What's your name," Jex asked the girl.

"I'm Dafnea," the girl replied.

"Dafnea, I don't think I'm going to make it home. You need to find my brother, Duggie...Duglas. Tell him I'm sorry. Take care of him."

Dafnea cried as she watched the bravest girl she'd ever met die right in front of her. She kept her promise to Jex and took care of Duggie. She'd never forget Jex's bravery and she vowed to live up to it every single day for the rest of her life.

Creature of Habit

Gary was a creature of habit. His routines were the same every single day, except for Sunday, thank you very much. Sunday was the day he did nothing but read the Sunday paper, nap, and read war history books. Everything in his sky-rise apartment was just so-so. Maids came to clean once a week, and his laundry was done and put away twice a week, organized and coded by color.

He woke up at six-forty-five each weekday morning to catch a cab to work. Driving his own vehicle was stressful, not to mention the fact that it saved him oodles of money by not having a car payment, maintenance, insurance, and any other expense associated with owning an automobile.

Gary was a stress-free, drama-free kind of gentleman. He steered clear of anything that brought on undue stress and drama like they were one of the seven plagues that God brought down on ancient Egypt.

On this particular Monday, when Gary's alarm went off at nine-forty-seven a.m., he panicked. He'd never overslept a day in his life! All of the thoughts of all of the possibilities came crashing down on him. He could lose his job, which could lead to him losing his apartment, his subscription to his weekly paper, and on, and on.

Gary ran to his closet to grab the clothes he'd selected the night before. They were gone! Quickly, he ran to his drawers to select his socks because everybody knows you build your outfit around your socks. He had socks, but none of them were the type that he wore, and they weren't organized or color coded!

Befuddled, Gary went to his kitchen to grab some coffee. On his way there, he went through his living room. He just so happened to look out of the floor-to-ceiling, wall length windows that had an excellent view of the city's skyline, and noticed that something was different. And off. He paused, went to the window, and looked again. Yes. It was definitely a different skyline. Gary wondered if he was having a mid-life crisis, or maybe a mental breakdown.

Running his fingers through his neatly coifed hair (he woke up that way), he walked over to the couch and sat down. He stared at his bare feet for a few moments. He slowly began looking up and noticed that there was someone sitting directly across from him. He had dark hair, green eyes, and a mischievous grin.

Gary held his hands up like a robbery was happening. "Whatever you want! Take it! It's yours!" Gary shouted at the stranger.

Amused, the grinning stranger replied, "Relax, man. I'm not here to rob you."

"You're not?" Gary was dumbfounded, but then, everything that had happened to him so far was dumbfounding.

"No! I'm here to change your life," the stranger mused.

"I don't need change in my life, but I appreciate your interest. Now, if you'll excuse me, I need to figure out how to fix everything here." Gary started to get up, but the stranger held up his hand and gestured for him to sit back down. Gary complied, which felt very odd to him.

"My name is Loki," the stranger announced. "I have turned your world upside down because, well, you needed it. Desperately."

Gary began to object, but Loki had stood up and began pacing. He planted himself behind the chair he'd just been seated in. "Gary, my friend. You are too stuck in your routine! All of these habits have turned you into a creature of sorts."

Gary was wary now. He didn't like this Loki very much at all. Gary didn't even believe in Norse mythology. This must be a mental breakdown that he was having.

"I know what you're thinking, Gary," Loki was clearly amused. "This isn't a mental breakdown. Not at all. You see, you have the rest of your day to show me that you can do things, shall we say, out of order."

Gary's face went pale. HIs routine was his flotation device. He couldn't swim without it.

"You have until midnight to show me you're capable," Loki said before disappearing from sight.

Gary sat there, stunned. His routine was comfort. His habits were security. He was forty-five and couldn't remember the last time he'd lived without his routine. Sure, his routine had to be modified over the years, changing from school to work, and then from one job or position to the next, but for as long as he could remember, he'd had a set routine. It made him successful in both school and work. He didn't know what he was going to do.

Gary went to his room again to get dressed. He picked out socks that didn't match each other, though it made him cringe to do it. He made sure his outfit didn't go with his socks, also painful. Once he was dressed, he noticed that one of his legs felt heavy. He pulled his trousers down to reveal an elephant's leg!

Cursing Loki, Gary went outside and found a newsstand. He bought a paper and sat on a park bench, with *people*, and began reading the paper. He noticed that his eyes felt different suddenly. He pulled out his phone and used the selfie-camera setting, which he'd never used in his life, to see his reflection. He nearly dropped his phone. He now had raccoon eyes!

Gary continued to change-things-up-but-not-really all day long until he was comprised of an elephant leg, a zebra leg, monkey arms, a cow's body, an eagle's beak/mouth, and a mouse's ears. Feeling defeated, and rightly so, he made his way back to his apartment. He was gawked at the entire way.

Loki met him in his apartment. "Tsk, tsk," Loki shook his head in mock shame. "You didn't really try, did ya, Gary? Well, I suppose now you'll have to remain, forever, a true creature of habit."

With that, Loki disappeared forever and Gary did, in fact, remain a creature of habit until the end of his days.

Personal Demons

Bondo, a college student from Japan, was studying at a university in the United States. Her classes required a big backpack for all of her books and they weighed heavy on her tiny frame.

Bondo was used to battling her personal demons and sometimes saw them with her reflection in windows and mirrors. Something she learned in one of her university classes was that when your personal demons are trying to tear you down, you can battle them with positivity. Think positive thoughts, say positive words. It had helped to keep them at bay, but it hadn't vanquished them forever.

There's no telling why this particular day was special, or particularly different from any other day, but this was the day that things began to change forever in Bondo's world. On this very unusual day, Bondo took the elevator up to her fourth-floor dorm room. She was in the elevator by herself, her earbuds in. They were repeating positive thoughts to battle the demons she'd noticed in the silvery reflection of the elevator doors.

The lights began to flicker. Bondo wasn't scared, but certainly intrigued. The doors to the elevator opened. Bondo was trapped inside the elevator and it was stuck between floors. Still not really panicked, she read the instructions for emergencies and alerted somebody that she was stuck in there between floors.

"I'm afraid it's going to be a while, miss. We'll have to make some calls, but we'll get someone there as soon as possible."

Bondo sighed, but decided she'd make the best of it. She was getting ready to sit down, pull out a book, and study, but there was somebody standing in the doorway of the elevator. He didn't look right, and this time, Bondo was a little bit spooked. That somebody was a personal demon she was quite familiar with.

"Hello, Bondo," the demon sneered.

"I know who you are," Bondo spat.

It was a demon that frequently tormented her. It told her that she wasn't smart and would never amount to anything. It made her re-think every word she ever said aloud because she was certain it came out wrong and that somebody would be offended or hurt. Its name was Self-Doubt.

"Good," it said. "We can skip introductions and move straight to torture."

"Not today, Self-Doubt," Bondo whined. "Can't you see I'm already stuck in this elevator? I don't need this now."

Self-Doubt didn't care. It began attacking her. It started with verbal assaults. The same ones she was used to. She imagined a shield, and it appeared. She didn't block every advance, but nearly. When its advances became more aggressive, the shield began to falter.

With each word that Self-Doubt hurled at Bondo she became weaker, falling to the floor. During the struggle her earbuds had come unplugged and she could hear the app on her phone giving her encouragement. Except, the voice on the app was her own. Her shield came back in full force. Along with it came a flaming sword.

Bondo found a new source of energy when she began to believe the words coming out of her mouth...umh, app. She attacked Self-Doubt with deliberate blows while shielding herself from its advances.

Just as she was about to finally dispatch Self-Doubt once and for all another of her personal demons showed up. Self-Doubt was lying in the floor, bloodied and bruised.

The new demon looked down at Self-Doubt and became enraged at seeing its brother in its current condition. This was one of Bondo's strongest and most overwhelming demons.

"Bondo," Shame said through gritted teeth.

Bondo was barely resisting the urge to cower in the corner. The shame of all of the mistakes she'd made over the years, her regrets... Shame heaped them on her like a pile of rocks. The weight was unbearable. She couldn't breathe, couldn't think. She was having a panic attack.

Somehow, the volume on her app became unnaturally loud and it began to lift the pile of shame from Bondo's shoulders as she listened and accepted her inner-app voice. Slowly, Bondo stood and met her attacker. She readied her stance, shield in one hand, flaming sword in the other.

Shame made the first move, but it was blocked easily by Bondo's shield. She retaliated with her flaming sword. They battled and battled for what felt like hours. Sweat was pouring from Bondo like she was responsible for flooding the Sahara Desert. At last, she struck a blow and Shame fell, landing on top of its brother.

Bondo stood over them, victory at hand as she grabbed the hilt of her sword with both hands. She lifted the sword high and then plunged the sword into the chests of the demons that were no longer hers. They crackled like a log in the fire, then disappeared in a puff of dirty smoke. Exhausted from the battles, Bondo reached in her bag for her water bottle. She took a big swig and sat down, forgetting that anyone was even supposed to be rescuing her from the elevator.

The lights flickered in the elevator again and the elevator doors closed. When she reached her floor, there was a man in laborers gear waiting for her.

"Are you alright, miss? You were in there for quite a while."

Bondo shrugged her backpack onto her tiny shoulders, contemplating the man's question.

"You know, I am good. Really, really good."

The man looked confused, but it didn't faze her. She smiled with pride and self-satisfaction on her way to her dorm room where she slept more peacefully than she had in years. She had other personal demons, but they weren't attacking her at the moment. Maybe word had gotten 'round that Bondo is a demon slayer.

The Loyalty of a Friend

Todd got out of his Corolla, locking the doors behind him. He walked up the sidewalk, past the shrubbery, and up to his front door with his paper bag of groceries in hand. Unlocking the door, he walked in on something very strange. His roommate, who also happened to be his best friend, was there. That wasn't the strange part. No, the strange part was that his friend, Larry, was wrestling two men dressed in all black suits, with white button-down shirts. They had sunglasses on. Inside.

Todd stood there and watched the wrestling for a moment, not sure what to do. He had no idea what was going on, or what Larry had gotten himself into. Larry was a quiet guy and not really the type to draw attention to himself. This added to the shock and awe of the prize fight happening before Todd's eyes.

All three of the wrestlers paused once they realized they were no longer alone. They all three stood up, brushing themselves off. Each of the men in suits blocked the only two exits out of the living room.

"Umh, Larry. What's goin' on, man?" Todd asked. Todd was often mistaken for being high, but he never touched any drugs. He was just naturally a slow talker.

"Larry?" one of the dark clad men asked in shock. "Your name isn't Larry. It's Larva, and you are here illegally!"

"What?" Todd asked. "You mean, he's not in America legally? Like, he made it over the President's wall?" Todd was confused. Larry didn't look Mexican.

The other suit probably rolled his eyes, but Todd couldn't tell for sure. Sunglasses.

"No, you moron. He's on this *planet* illegally. He's from the planet Nondura. He's a slave on the run and he must be sent back to his planet," suit number one exclaimed.

Todd was confused. "Larry, you're from a different planet?"

Larry nodded, hanging his head in shame. "I'm sorry I didn't tell you, man. I just didn't want to get you involved. That worked out well, huh?"

Todd nodded, deep in thought. Well, deep for Todd. "So, you have to take Larry back to his planet?" he asked the suits.

They nodded in unison.

"I don't know how this works, but what if I could vouch for him being here. If I can show that he's been a good citizen of this planet, can he stay?"

"If he'd come here legally, after legally terminating his slave contract with his owner, there wouldn't be an issue. The fact of the matter is that he didn't do either of those things and now we have to return him," suit number two said firmly.

"But we abolished slavery!" Todd shouted. He was beginning to panic and he was getting desperate.

Suit number one sighed. "Yes, we abolished slavery in this country, but what happens on Nondura is none of our business. Our agreement with the Galactical Parliament is to honor their laws when we have one of their criminals, and that's what we're going to do."

"It's ok, Todd," Larry said in resignation. "They're right. I need to go and take care of things on Nondura, and with any luck, I'll be back."

Todd dropped his bag of groceries on the floor. "Sirs, is it alright if I have a moment with Larry? He's been my best friend for a long time. and my roommate. I'd like to say a proper goodbye."

The suits looked at each other, annoyed, but understanding. They nodded at Todd, giving him their blessing.

"We'll just be right over here," Todd said, indicating the entryway to the kitchen from the living room.

Both of the suits stood by the front door.

Todd hugged Larry, making sure his head was on Larry's shoulder that the suits couldn't see. "Larry," he whispered, "as an alien, can you do any cool things that we humans aren't capable of?"

Larry nodded his head and whispered, "I can replicate myself. The replica dissipates after about ten minutes."

Todd had a plan, which was surprising. He didn't usually find himself in need of one. "Larry, make a replica and have your replica run out through the open window in the living room while I'm talking to you, but you stay here."

Larry did as Todd suggested and, out of nowhere, a replica of Larry showed up in the living room. The replica barely dodged the suits, but made it out the window. The suits chased after him. Larry and Todd let out a quiet shout of joy and surprise. Who knew a plan of Todd's would actually work?

"Larry, leave your phone, and all of your things here," Todd said. "You have to run and go somewhere they won't expect you. If you sense them on your trail, make replicas to get those suits off your back."

Larry gave Todd one more hug. "You're the best friend I've ever had, Todd. I won't forget you."

"Same here, man," Todd said. He was trying not to cry. He thought he'd save it for later and eat his feelings while watching crazy old black and white movies.

And with that, Todd and Larry forever parted. Todd never knew what became of Larry, whether he got picked up, or made a new life for himself somewhere else on this planet. Todd took solace in the fact that he'd had years with Larry and that Todd had been loyal to his best friend to the very end. Todd became more active in the cause for immigration, both on this planet and abroad. He never married because he was married to the cause. On occasion, Todd thought he felt Larry watching him. Maybe from behind a tree, or across a road. It warmed his heart to think so.

Living in Her Shadow

"I'm tired of living in your shadow!" Those were the last words that Jaclyn had heard from her little sister, Marissa, before she stormed off into the rain three days ago.

Their parents had certainly put a lot of pressure on both of the girls to succeed. Jaclyn felt like she received the most pressure because she was the oldest and was required to set an example for Marissa.

Marissa felt like she was under the most pressure because she had to live up to all of Jaclyn's accolades. They'd been fighting over who had the most pressure before Marissa walked away, perhaps forever.

Jaclyn paused to stretch near a concrete building while on her usual morning walk. Her shadow stretched with her on the wall of the building. When she was finished, she started to walk away, but she noticed that her shadow didn't move with her. She went back to where she finished stretching and tried leaving again, but her shadow did not budge. Puzzled, Jaclyn scratched her head and stared at her shadow on the concrete wall.

"I won't go with you. Not until you get Marissa to stop living here. I'm not a residence to be lived in," her shadow said to her. It sounded a lot like Jaclyn, but it was muffled a little bit.

"I'm sorry...what?" Jaclyn asked, confused.

"I will *not* be going with you! Marissa is right. She can no longer live in your shadow...*me*. She needs to shine in her own light! Until you rectify the situation, I quit!" The shadow detached itself from Jaclyn and ran up the wall, disappearing out of sight.

Jaclyn walked back home, dazed and confused. She thought about the consequences of not having a shadow. It wouldn't be so bad, would it? Then she thought about how people would react if they realized that she didn't cast a shadow. She didn't live in the days of the Salem Witch Trials, but it would freak people out.

When she arrived home, she flopped onto her bed and thought things over. It was silly, really. The fight she'd had with Marissa. Who cares who is under more pressure? Mom and Dad always put crazy pressure on both of them to perform. They'd be stronger working together, rather than against each other. Jaclyn sat up and grabbed her phone, dialing her sister's number.

"Hello?" Marissa answered.

"Hey, Riss. It's Jaclyn. Don't hang up! I just wanted to say that I'm sorry about the other day. Can you come over for lunch? I'll make your favorite...Caprese salad."

"Jaclyn, I'm not sure..." her voice trailed off.

"I promise, I don't want to fight and I'm not going to demand that I'm right, either."

Marissa sighed. "Okay. Is noon good for you?

"Noon is perfect!" Jaclyn said. "See you then!"

"Yeah, see you," Marissa sighed again.

Jaclyn showered, and went to the store, buying up all of the ingredients needed for Marissa's favorite meal. She bought flowers for her sister and a carefully selected apology card. When she got to the register, the cashier was rather chatty.

"Uh-oh. This looks like an apology meal," he said. "What'd you do?"

Not that it was any of his business, but Jaclyn replied anyway, "It's less of an apology, and more of a peace negotiation that involves an apology."

The cashier chuckled. "Uh-huh. Okay. Good luck with that. It'll be thirty-three dollars and eighty-nine cents."

Jaclyn paid for her items and rushed home to prepare everything. She set the table with her fancy plates and flatware, linen napkins and tablecloth, and set the flowers and the card in the center of the table. She made Earl Grey, Marissa's favorite tea, and put it on the table with her tea set. Everything was ready and in place for her lunch with Marissa.

Marissa let herself in and Jaclyn hugged her, which was awkward for both of them because they almost never hugged each other. Jaclyn decided that she would tell her sister what she had been thinking before they ate lunch so that they could just enjoy the meal and not have all of this tension.

"Marissa, I'm sorry about our fight the other day. I have a lot to say and I really hope you will hear me out," Jaclyn said.

Marissa nodded her head and waited for Jaclyn to begin.

"Mom and Dad have always put so much pressure on the both of us and it's never been fair to either of us. My pressure is not greater than yours, it's just different. Rather than letting the pressure get to me, I've decided that I'm going to just be here for you and try to absorb some of your pressure with you because you deserve to shine on your own without being compared to anyone. Especially me."

A tear formed in Jaclyn's eye.

"I'm so, so sorry I let the pressure come between us. We should be a safety net for each other, not a death trap."

Both girls chuckled a little at Jaclyn's last line. Marissa, tears streaming down her face, responded. "Jaclyn, I'm sorry too. You're right. We should be safety nets for each other, and our pressures are different, not greater than or less than. I can't express how much it means to me that you reached out to me like this. Though I have been tired of living in your shadow, I have always looked up to you. I hope that we can work this out and become close friends."

The girls hugged and cried a little.

As they stood up to move into the dining room, Marissa said, "Oh, yeah. Your shadow found me. It told me that I couldn't live in it anymore and that I was going to have to figure out a different arrangement."

Jaclyn laughed. "It told me the same thing and that's what got me thinking about it all. I hope it returns to me soon, but even if it doesn't, what I said still stands."

The girls laughed and enjoyed their first lunch together as best friends.

Zombie Sacrifice

Al saw them coming, though the sun hadn't provided much light. It was barely sunrise and the zombies were already up and at it. It had been a while since they'd been to his neighborhood and he'd become comfortable. He had maybe one minute, two at best to gather what he needed and get out the back door before they came to his house to search for some brain food.

He grabbed his last two bottles of purified water, some granola bars, toilet paper, his two favorite books, some ammo, and a sawed-off shotgun. Just as he grabbed the gun he heard the zombies trying to break down his front door. He ran out the back door, through his yard, and out the back of it into an empty alley. He may have missed the zombies, but not by much. It wouldn't take them long to follow his scent to the alley. Al cursed as he realized that he'd forgotten his bottle of deer urine. It smelled horrible, but it was pretty effective in getting zombies off of your scent. They weren't interested in animals.

Al made a run for it, thinking maybe he could find some deer urine at the next abandoned convenience store. It was a best seller after the zombies became a problem and before his little town of three thousand became a ghost town.

At fifty-eight years old, Al was not in the best of shape. He'd been in decent shape in the military, but he'd been retired almost twenty years and never bothered to keep up with his fitness regimen.

By the time he got to the convenience store, Al was rather winded. He stopped just outside the glass double doors, broken through some time ago. He took a moment to catch his breath, keeping his eyes and ears alert. Finally, he entered the convenience store, looking for some deer urine. He found some and tossed about half a dozen bottles into his bag. He'd leave money for it, but money was of no use in this town. There wasn't really anybody to exchange it with.

Al went on his way. He'd discovered some time back that the zombies, crazy as they were, had a sort of system. They would hunt in certain areas of town and move on when there was nothing left for them to eat, or if supply was simply too scarce. He knew of a subdivision that he could go to where he would be safe for a little while, so he made his way there. He found a house that still had lights, heat, and hadn't seen any real damage. He picked the lock, entered the house, and made himself at home.

Hungry and thirsty after his hasty excursion, Al pulled out a granola bar and a bottle of water. He popped in a DVD from the collection that was there, turned on the tv, and watched as he ate. A few minutes later, a boy who couldn't be any older than nine or ten came out of the hallway with a baseball bat. Al wasn't scared in the slightest, but he didn't want to scare the boy either. He put up his hands and said, "Hey, there."

"Are...are you a zombie?" the boy yelled, bat raised like he was going to hit a home run. He was trying to sound brave, but the fear in his voice told a different story.

"No. Are you?" Al asked, knowing that the boy wasn't. If the boy was a zombie, they wouldn't be exchanging words.

"No," the boy answered. "What are you doing in my house?"

"Same as you, I expect. I'm Al, and I just ran across town to get away from some zombies. What's your name?"

The boy hesitated, not sure he could trust anyone.

"It's alright, son. I'm not going to hurt you."

The boy lowered his bat, but still held on to it, just in case. "I'm Levi."

"Levi, huh? How old are you?" Al asked him.

"Ten. I've been taking care of myself for a couple of years now," he said, chin held high.

"Ten? I thought you were twelve the way you came out here with that bat," Al said, trying to gain Levi's trust.

Levi raised one eyebrow in a smirk that said he saw right through Al.

Al offered Levi a granola bar and the other bottle of water. Slowly, Levi accepted, and sat on the opposite end of the couch from Al.

Out of nowhere, a swarm of zombies flooded the living room through the kitchen. They'd gotten stealthier, getting into the house without Al or Levi detecting them. Al dropped his food and water, grabbed his pack, and started to take off.

Levi sat in panic.

Al was tempted to leave him. He'd been alone for so long, it didn't feel natural to be responsible for anyone again. Al grabbed Levi's arm and pulled him to his feet. Levi followed and they made it down the hall into the master bedroom where they locked themselves inside.

Al rummaged through his pack and grabbed a couple of bottles of deer urine. He opened one and drenched Levi in it. Levi resisted at first, but Al insisted, quickly explaining what it does.

Al gave Levi his pack and helped him out of the window when the zombies burst through the door. Al told Levi to run and to find a safe place. He said that if he made it out alive, he'd catch up to him.

Al knew that he wouldn't make it out alive and, somehow, Levi did too. He did as he was told, and left Al there with his shotgun to accept his fate.

Fallen Soldier

John had never felt so lost in his life. He'd been living on his own in the woods for the last few months and life was never harder. He missed his parents, his friends, and everyone else he cared about when North Korea bombed the United States four months ago.

Everyone had thought that the washed-up athlete could negotiate peace between the countries. As usual, the citizens of the United States were sorely misguided. Not that he thought the President could have done any better, but what did he know? He was just some twenty-three-year-old kid without a home, a job, or a family.

There was so much devastation in the fallout that anyone had hardly recognized that Fall had made its appearance, nearly giving way to winter. John walked through the forest, the crunch of fallen leaves calling to him from below his military booted feet. His latest kill was slung over his shoulder as he headed back to his hut. He had a habit of stopping about a mile out from the hut to make sure nobody was following him. So far, so good.

John reached his hut and immediately began to clean the game he'd killed for supper. He needed to prepare it and get his fire going before the early sunset. He put some logs in his fire pit and was ready to start the fire when he heard the noise of leaves crunching again. The sound wasn't from him and it didn't sound like an animal. John grabbed the knife he'd used to clean his kill and searched the perimeter, eyes wide, breathing shallow.

A Korean soldier came out from behind a tree and was startled by John's appearance. John had a military build and was holding a bloody knife. In broken English, the Korean soldier attempted to communicate with him. He tried to tell John that he wasn't there to hurt him. The soldier put his own hands up in surrender, tears streaming down his face. He had something in his hands and he offered it to John.

Keeping his knife at the ready, John reached out and accepted what the soldier was showing him. A baby girl. A woman, probably the soldier's wife.

The soldier didn't even bother to appear brave. He wanted John to understand. He was done with this war and wanted to go home to his family.

"This is your wife?" John asked. The soldier nodded vigorously. "And your daughter?" The soldier nodded again as he began to sob. John had no pity for this man. Was this the soldier who dropped the bomb that killed his family? Even if he wasn't, he represented the regime that did this to him.

"You expect me to let you go so you can go back to your family?" John shouted. "Do you know what your country has done to *my* family?!"

The soldier hung his head.

This man was clearly not aggressive, but again, John couldn't find it in him to care. John twirled the handle of his knife over and over in his hand, anger and bitterness flooding him again as he remembered coming home to find that all his family were dead. John never considered himself a murderer, and though he'd like to see North Korea pay for its crimes, he just didn't have it in him to do the job.

John threw the pictures on the ground at the soldier's feet.

The soldier picked it up and began to back away slowly.

Out of nowhere, John heard a bunch of men running in their direction. They were U.S. Military and they had spotted the Korean soldier. John didn't make a move. He neither aided in the soldier's capture, nor in his attempt at escape. The U.S. soldiers yelled for the North Korean soldier to stop and put his hands in the air, but he didn't listen.

John was close enough to hear the man as he lay dying. He told John that if he were caught, he wouldn't be allowed to go home. At least if he died in combat, his wife and daughter would have something proud to remember him by. John tried really hard not to let the words of this dying North Korean soldier get to him, but he was unsuccessful. The American soldiers apologized to John for disrupting his day and that they'd be taking the dead soldier with them.

He watched as they carried him off unceremoniously. When they were no longer in sight, John looked down and found the pictures that the dead soldier had dropped when he'd been shot. He thought he'd feel some sense of justice, or vengeance, or *something*. John hit a nearby tree with his fist. He might as well have been the one to kill the guy himself for all the good it did him. And now, imagining that poor little girl growing up without her daddy just made him sick to his stomach. If he'd already eaten, he almost certainly would have vomited right there.

     That day was the hardest day of his life, second only to losing his family. John continued living in the woods where he remained alone. Each day became a little easier for him to go on, though he never forgot about the Korean's wife and daughter. He said a prayer for them every day, hoping that they were okay and unashamed of the man who died to protect their dignity. Every day was a new opportunity to find peace and forgiveness for himself, as well as the others who were both the enemy and sad casualties of an unnecessary war.

A Husband's Dream

    Willard sat at Alma's bedside in the nursing home. His bride of nearly 70 years, his partner, his friend. He'd been awake with her since he'd arrived early that morning, and only left her side to use the restroom. The staff brought meals and snacks to him throughout the day, knowing that he wouldn't eat otherwise. Not that he had much of a stomach for food at the moment. Willard had been having some health issues of his own and it meant that he couldn't stomach very many kinds of food.

    It was getting close to eleven at night and Willard was getting very sleepy. He knew that Alma could go at any second and he wanted to be there and be alert when it happened. He wanted her to have his full attention, all the way to the end. Holding her hand, he laid his head back in his chair. Tears began to make trails down his wrinkled face as he remembered all of the good times with Alma. They'd never had children, so they were all each other had left in the world, and he couldn't have been happier.

    He found himself taking a trip down memory lane. Alma was there, on his arm as they walked through the crisp, cool autumn air. The old streetlamps were lit, and they each had their long coats on with gloves, caps, and scarves. They were young in this memory, and they felt like the only two people in the world when they were together. Most of their dates ended with a walk, regardless of the weather. Except perhaps for rain, or a heavy snow.

    They continued their walk for quite some time, laughing and enjoying each other's company. They came upon a small church and, to Willard's surprise, it was the church that he and Alma were married in.

    Next thing he knew, he and Alma were facing each other, still young, but now dressed in a suit and gown. This was the day that Alma made him the happiest man on Earth. The day she took him to be her husband. They didn't have grand plans for the future, like all the kids seem to want nowadays. They didn't care what their future held, so long as they were in that future together.

Willard tried desperately to remember something he'd forgotten. Something that tugged at his brain like a child wanting his mother's attention. They kissed after the minister pronounced them man and wife, and they ran from the church, happier than they'd ever been. They drove off into the sunset in Willard's beat up vehicle.

Suddenly, Willard and Alma were still driving in the car, but they weren't in their wedding attire. Instead, they were in funeral attire. They were on their way to the funeral of Alma's last living relative; her mother. Willard's heart broke for Alma in that moment just as it had the day it actually happened. They had already lost his parents, and Alma had no siblings. Her father had died a few years earlier. Just like with everything else in life, they leaned on each other and made it through.

They got back in the car and drove away. They drove to a doctor's office where their attire changed again. They were in their Sunday's best, hoping to receive good news from the doctor. The doctor didn't have good news for Willard and Alma. In fact, the news was heartbreaking. The doctor broke the news that they weren't going to be able to have children. It devastated them. They didn't have treatments for it back then like they do today, so they just had to learn how to accept it and move on.

It wasn't easy. Alma fell into a depression for a few years after receiving the news. Willard's patience, love, and understanding brought healing for Alma's broken heart, and they learned to be happy again.

Willard couldn't shake the feeling that he had something he was supposed to be remembering. Something, maybe, he should be doing. What was it? It was going to bother him all night until he figured it out.

Willard was brought back to his memories of his life with Alma, but he'd ended up skipping several years. The year he retired. They'd lived modestly and it allowed them to travel together when Willard reached retirement. The look on Alma's face when they first set foot on the beach in Italy was worth every extra hour he had to work over the course of his life. Traveling brought Alma joy and, what made his wife happy, made him ecstatic. Especially when he was the one providing it.

Willard and Alma were lying on the beach in Italy when he turned to Alma and said,

"You know, I keep having this feeling that there's something I've forgotten. Maybe something I forgot to do. Any ideas?"

"No, Willard, dear. I can't think of anything besides lying here on the beach with you," Alma said sweetly.

It occurred to Willard in that moment. He was sleeping, and he desperately needed to wake up. Alma wasn't lying on a beach, she was lying in her bed at the nursing home. If he didn't wake up, he might miss out on being with her till the very end. He started to get up, but his backside seemed to be glued to the seat.

"Where are you going, dear?" Alma asked him.

"This is a dream," he said. "I'm asleep and, in the real world, you're dying."

"Don't be silly, Willard," Alma said. "We're both gone, and this is where we get to spend eternity. Isn't it lovely?"

It was true. Willard and Alma had slipped into blissful eternity at just the same time. He and Alma enjoyed their retirement on the beach in Italy for all of eternity.

A Dream Come True

Anne wondered what she could have done differently. She was hiding in the trees watching her family...no, her former family, play in the park as the sun was setting. She had been trying to figure out what had brought her to this place. Not the park, but the place in her life where she had to watch her family from a distance, like some sort of creepy stalker.

She thought about how miserable she'd been during her last days with her family. Anxiety and depression had plagued her for years and it had affected everything. She couldn't work because the idea of it nearly brought on a panic attack. Not working meant less money in the bank, and because her anxiety and depression sometimes made her shop compulsively, that meant what little money they had was going down an irreversible drainage system.

Her poor husband tried to bear as much of the weight as he could. She recognized it, but was afraid to acknowledge it aloud. She feared he would think that because she saw and understood the need, she would be able to pick herself up by the bootstraps and go out and get a job. The truth was, she thought about it *all the time*. She hated seeing her family financially strapped, her husband worrying about the bills, and her not being able to contribute any kind of support.

One night, she'd been thinking about all of this as she went to bed for the evening. Sometimes, to get her mind to focus on one thing that wasn't important, she would silently tell herself a story. That night, she told herself a story about vampires. Well, one vampire in particular.

His name was Desmond. He was handsome, mysterious and, for whatever reason, he thought she was attractive. It was her story, so she went with it. She had a wonderful time with Desmond. He'd asked her about her life, her family. She explained her family's situation. Explained her illnesses and the affect it had on the family.

"I can help you make all of that go away," Desmond said.

Excited that this might be a passionate night like she hadn't known in a very long time, she took the bait.

"I can show you," he said, "but, you have to give me permission first."

Anne nodded her head, giving her assent.

Desmond kissed her throat. "Is this ok?" Desmond asked, his voice sultry and dangerous.

Anne nodded assent again, feeling like she might faint.

"Tell me," he said, "tell me it's ok."

"It's ok, Desmond," Anne breathed.

Desmond kissed her neck one more time before sinking his vampire teeth into her bulging vein. He drank in ecstasy. She remembered. She could feel his ecstasy, and feel it becoming her own. He nearly drank her dry. She recalled feeling his lack of self-control.

Desmond regained control just in time, panting like he'd just run a marathon. "You must be famished," he said to Anne, looking at her pale skin. Here," he said, "drink."

Desmond slit his wrist, allowing Anne to drink from him. He was right. She felt famished. Anne's mind was repulsed, but her body craved it. She drank from Desmond's wrist until she couldn't anymore.

Anne remembered waking up from that dream in her own bed, lying next to her husband. That was the best night's sleep she'd had in a long time. She felt refreshed, alert, and ready to do anything. She even considered applying for a job later that day.

She might have actually done it, but when she went into the bathroom and began brushing her hair, she noticed two holes in her neck. She touched them gingerly. They were tender to the touch.

Anne found herself in a sort of haze. Last night was a dream she'd concocted. How could it have been real? Anne hid her neck with scarves or turtlenecks. Technically it was fall, but they were still experiencing summer weather where she lived, so the scarves and turtlenecks were a dead giveaway that she was hiding something. Her poor husband thought she was having an affair, no matter how many times she assured him otherwise.

As the days went by the wound began to heal, but Anne started craving blood. She could smell it when people walked by her, even her own family were tempting to her taste buds.

Appalled by this, Anne thought there was only one thing to do. She had to figure out who Desmond was and how to fix this. She'd wanted a temporary escape, not a nightmare ending to an already bad situation.

Anne drove to the nearest cemetery that night, walking alone among the graves. She sensed Desmond before she saw him. He still made her blush when he looked at her.

"I knew you'd come here to find me eventually," he said softly, with a hint of hope in his voice.

"How did you do it, Desmond? I was dreaming, and you were a made-up character in the story I wrote for myself. How did I wake up so...different?" Anne was desperate for answers. Even more desperate for a solution.

"If I told you, would I remain your mysterious lover?" Desmond asked with a smirk.

"Desmond, you don't understand. My anxiety and depression have gone away, but my family... I can't stay like this with my family, but I can't leave them either. They're going through so much already...they'd be devastated if I have to leave. How do we reverse this?"

"I can see that you are not up to speed on your lore," Desmond said. "But, this is irreversible, darling. I know it's hard, because I've been there." He put a hand on her shoulder. "It's time to say goodbye to your old life, and a warm, hardy 'Hello' to your new life with me."

Anne spent the rest of the night bawling her eyes out while Desmond held her and wiped her tears away. She'd never forget the hurt she watched her family go through when she left. She'd trade anything to have it all back. The bills, the illnesses, her family, all of it.

Desmond called her down from the tree she was perched in, watching her former family in the park. She hopped down, taking one last look before walking away forever into her new life that she never wanted, but definitely dreamed about.

Teen Parenthood

Zoe woke up feeling devastated by the news of her father's recent passing. She had this feeling in the pit of her stomach that her life was about to change forever. At the age of sixteen she had taken on a motherly role for her younger siblings, Otto and Grace, years ago. Otto was fourteen, and Grace was eleven.

Both parents lived in the home, but the father usually had his eyes glued to the TV. He was still the parent of choice because he didn't abuse and manipulate the children, like their mother did. Their father could sometimes be convinced to play a game with them once in a while, or go out for something fun like ice cream or pizza.

With their father gone, and their mother the way she was, Zoe felt a heavy burden of responsibility to take care of Otto and Grace. There was no way she could live with her mother now that her father was gone, since he usually acted as a sort of buffer when he was home. And since Zoe couldn't stay, she couldn't leave her siblings there in that terrible house. She wouldn't abandon them the way their father had unintentionally abandoned them all.

Zoe's brain worked furiously through all of the options. If the government got a hold of the three of them, they would be split up. Nobody wants to take a sixteen-year-old kid, and fewer want to take in a group of three siblings. Splitting up was not an option.

Zoe would have to get a job, find a way to finish school, and find a place for them to live. The tasks ahead of her were daunting, overwhelming her with a sense of foreboding. Could she really take all of this on? She made meals for her siblings more often than not anyway. Maybe she could go live with her grandparents? No, her mother would never allow it.

Zoe sat on her bed, crying as quietly as possible. If there was something, anything her mother wouldn't tolerate, it was someone being a loud blubbering mess - no matter the circumstance. Everything felt so impossible. So *crazy* impossible. She thought about how Otto and Grace would react to the news. Her mother hadn't even shed a tear. Not a single one. She hadn't shown any sympathy towards her children for losing their father either. Would Otto and

Grace want to go with her? Would they accept her as their new parental authority, or would they want to stay with their mom and tough it out?

One thing Zoe knew for sure was that they would need to stick around for the funeral. She knew that she and her siblings would all need the closure attending a funeral can provide. They might even have to stick around longer than that. She would need to get a job and save up for a place to live and a vehicle. She didn't even have her license yet. Her mother was of the mind that she couldn't get a car and her license until she got a job, but she needed a car to get to work because they lived out in the middle of nowhere. Maybe she could catch a ride from some friends at school. She hated relying on the kindness of others to make her responsibility a possible concept, but she was beginning to feel desperate.

Zoe was exhausted. Thinking all of this through, taking on the responsibility of two adults for two kids when she was still a kid herself nearly had her sticking one foot in the grave. She could almost feel gray hairs sprouting on her head, wrinkles setting in from worry and stress.

She hated her parents in that moment. She hated them for putting her in this position. If they had been half decent parents, Zoe wouldn't have near as much to worry about. She was most angry with her mother. Her mother should be worried about her children. Wondering how they're handling the news. Comforting them, even if she isn't sad for herself.

Instead, she was likely worried about the insurance policy, and how soon she could collect it. She'd burn through it in no time buying things that she doesn't need, yet make her feel and look important. Even at sixteen, if Zoe had received the policy funds, she would buy a small home, a modest vehicle, and put some away for other bills so she wouldn't have to work while she and her siblings finished school. Thinking about all of this just made her more and more upset.

Zoe took a deep breath and laid back down. It was beginning to dawn on her that her father had not died in a car accident. It was one of those dreams that feels *so* real. The emotions were real, the needs that arose from the situation were real. Zoe cried again with fresh tears. She felt a little foolish for going through all of that heartache when it was just a dream. Mostly, she felt a huge relief. Though she was already a sort of surrogate mother to Otto and Grace, she didn't have to take on all of the other responsibilities after all.

    Zoe finished her cry and went to the bathroom to wash up. She used cool water to take the swelling down around her eyes before heading back to her room to get dressed and ready for the day. She went downstairs and gave her dad, who was very much alive, a huge hug. It wasn't totally out of the ordinary, so her father didn't think about it too much. Zoe went on with her day and her life, appreciating the fact that she didn't have to be so heavily burdened with a task that shouldn't be hers, even if she was already a bit of a teenage parent, and a pretty darn good one at that.

Choices

Dani woke up one morning with an unusual spring in her step. Maybe it was the great night's sleep she got the night before, she didn't really know. She had a habit of just running with whatever she was feeling in the moment, never caring to examine why she felt that way, let alone journal about it or log it somehow. She had better things to do, theoretically. She had loads of shows to catch up on, movies she hadn't seen. Oh, and the books that she'd been meaning to read, but never got around to somehow.

Yes, Dani definitely had better things to do than to sit around for a whole five minutes and journal about her feelings, examining the things that might have led her to feel that way. The trouble was, Dani allowed her feelings to direct her. So, if someone yelled at her that day, it meant the whole day was ruined. However, if her crush told her he liked her, then the entire day was a win. Unless, of course, both bad things and good things happened that day, then she had a tendency to run with the negative feelings of what happened that day, and calling the whole day a bad one.

If Dani had journaled about these things, she would have noticed these patterns. But then, what would she have done about it? The fact that her feelings dictated what kind of day she was having was a strong thing to come up against - like big, crushing waves for someone stranded in the middle of the ocean with no flotation device, not knowing how to swim.

Nevertheless, she continued with her day, feeling wonderful until something happened. It was difficult, and she didn't like that she had to deal with it. It was somebody she had to deal with every single school day. Two somebodies, really. See, Dani had a couple of girls that hated her. They were sisters and they just really loved picking on Dani. They never touched her, never pushed her physically. But they always made awful remarks about Dani each time they saw her. And they saw her often. Dani had classes with at least one of the sisters a few times a day, and she rode the bus with them too. No matter how great her day started, Dani usually let these sisters get her down. They were so mean, and she really had never done anything to deserve it. Dani tried to push it out of her head, but she was always unsuccessful and it would almost always ruin her day.

Fortunately for Dani, her bus driver took notice. He told her, "Dani, those girls have made a choice. They have decided that they are going to be snide, mean bullies. The great news is that you get to choose who you're going to be as well. Are you going to make the choice to let their shenanigans get you down? Are you going to decide to let what they say and do make a difference in your daily life? Are you going to give them that kind of power? Or are you going to not let their crazy seep into your day? Are you going to choose to be joyful and content in spite of their attacks?"

Dani was taken aback. She thanked her bus driver, who'd always been kind to her, and then left the bus to walk home. He'd left her with a lot to consider.

When she got home she decided that she would get a notebook out and make a list of the things she would choose to be. Her list was long, which made her proud. It included things like: kind, forgiving, joyful, content, empathetic, and so much more. It was in that moment that Dani realized that she wanted more out of life and that she was tired of other people and circumstances deciding her life for her. She was going to begin deciding for herself.

The next day was tough. She was aware that she was going to be making choices throughout the day that would empower her to be in charge of her own life. It was just much harder than she imagined it would be. When she ran into the sisters on the bus, she had decided that she would pay them a compliment on a piece of clothing they were wearing, beating them to the punch. Confused, they stared at each other before turning back to Dani and snarling. They left her alone the rest of the bus ride to school. It had taken a lot of gumption, but Dani did it, and she was proud of herself.

Dani kept doing things like this when it came to those sisters and things slowly got better. She had a math class with the older sister. Dani was often finished with her math before anyone else, so her teacher asked her to walk around answering questions from the other students while the teacher worked on grading homework. The older sister raised her hand, asking for help. Reluctantly, Dani went over to her and asked her what her question was. Dani could see where the older sister was getting hung up and explained it to her in a way she felt the older sister could understand, and it worked.

Her face lit up. She asked Dani, "Why have you been so nice to us? And helping me with my math?"

Dani replied, "I believe in being kind, so I am." Dani smiled at the sister with true kindness and received an appreciative smile in return.

She didn't have any further trouble with those sisters after that day. In fact, if anyone else gave Dani a hard time, they would stick up for Dani. They even saved her a seat as close to them as possible on the bus each day. The day her bus driver intervened was the first day of Dani owning her life and *choosing* who she will be.

Together

"I just can't do this anymore, James." Sherry sighed as she rubbed her temples with the fingers and thumb of her right hand. They'd been fighting for months, and over so many things, she didn't even remember what started it all.

"You can't do this anymore?" James shouted at Sherry. In his mind, what "started it all" was actually the thing that just opened up the flood gates. Things had been piling up for years, and now that the dam had burst, he was ready to just let it all out.

"You know what I mean, James," Sherry's shoulders slumped with exhaustion. "The fighting has to stop," she looked up at him, a hard drink in her hand now. "One way or another," she finished, before downing her drink.

"We fight, and you immediately jump to divorce?" James yelled. His head spun with the overwhelming rush of feelings his heart had endured over the months of fighting.

"What I'm saying, James, is that it has to stop. I don't know what that will take. Worst case scenario would be divorce, but I don't want to do that until we've exhausted other resources," Sherry explained with more empathy in her voice. She really did want it to work.

James stopped pacing at the sad tone Sherry's voice had taken. It sort of snapped him out of his wild rollercoaster ride of emotions. "What sort of resources?"

Sherry set her empty glass on the coffee table and leaned back on the couch. "I think counseling is our best bet. What do you think about that?"

James was not interested in seeing a counselor. Not in the slightest. It would be the ultimate defeat. The ultimate removal of his manhood. It would mean that he wasn't capable of holding his marriage together and he just wasn't sure he could ever live with that. He told Sherry as much.

She resisted the urge to roll her eyes. "James, listen. Isn't *divorce* the ultimate defeat, indicating that you weren't able to hold your marriage together? It's the twenty-first century and this is what people do when they need to fix a broken relationship now."

James remained quiet, still not convinced that this was the right path.

"What if this is the only way to save our marriage? Is our marriage worth saving?"

"Of course, it's worth saving, Sherry," James said as he took a seat in the accent chair across from his wife.

"If it's worth saving, then doesn't that mean we should save it? At any cost?" Sherry let the question hang in the air, allowing James to put two and two together.

"You're right," James answered. "I just need some time to wrap my head around it."

Sherry nodded and scooted forward to the edge of her seat, resting her elbows on her knees. "I get that, and that's fine," she replied softly. "How about we take a week for both of us to wrap our heads around it, agree not to fight in the meantime, and then we'll work together on selecting a counselor."

James nodded, leaning his head against the back of his chair. "What happened to us, Sherry? We were amazing. I want us to be amazing again."

Sherry stood up from her seat on the couch and walked across the room to her husband. She kissed him on top of the head and answered softly, "I know, babe. I do too." She grabbed her empty glass from the table and took it into the kitchen to rinse it out.

Overwhelmed with emotions, primarily the sadness and reality of where their marriage stood, Sherry began to sob. She dropped the glass into the sink where it broke into a few pieces. She covered her eyes with one hand, her other hand holding her steady at the counter. She sobbed uncontrollably for a few minutes before she felt familiar arms wrap around her lower torso.

James was comforting her. They'd just been fighting, and he was comforting her. The gesture made her sob even harder, so he turned her around to face him and just held her. "I know," he whispered. "We both want this to work, and we'll make every last effort to get there. That's what matters right now." As he said it, he believed it. He felt the conviction of it deep in his bones. "Let's go to bed," James whispered, grabbing his wife's hand.

Sherry nodded and let her husband lead her to the bedroom. He got the bed ready while she freshened up her face and changed into her pajamas. The gesture nearly made her lose it again, but she gained control of herself quickly, climbing into bed. She thanked him for everything he'd done that evening. They both fell asleep quickly, dreaming of a brighter future together.

A few weeks later James and Sherry walked out of their first counseling appointment. The counselor had promised that there would be a lot of hard work, a lot of exhausting vulnerability, and a lot of patience and forgiveness ahead if they wanted to save their marriage. He'd told them that it would take a fair amount of time to heal the marriage, and that if they truly wanted to repair things, they would have to be in it for the long haul. They both came away from their counseling session with the first glimmer of hope they'd seen in a long time. For the first time in quite a while, they were on the road to a whole and fulfilling life, and they were headed that direction together.

Accepting a Werewolf

Seth was feeling particularly apathetic during the full moon phase. He was tired of the cycle. The never-ending cycle of hunting during a full moon and then going back to his human life where nobody seemed to suspect what he was.

He'd been a werewolf for over a century and had lived in a few different countries to keep his secret hidden. He was tired of making friends who became like family to him, knowing he'd have to leave them one day. He was still aging, but slowly. The process was slow enough that it would appear to his friends in each village as though he hadn't aged at all. His blood family all dead, Seth sought a home wherever he could find one.

He was currently living in a small village in Wales, where he'd been for about ten years. It was nearly time to move on, but he wasn't sure he could stomach another move. He'd grown very fond of the little village, and would stay there forever if he could. In fact, he was contemplating it one night.

He was tired of hiding, and pretending, and keeping secrets. He considered telling his best friend, Oliver, what he was. He scoffed at the idea immediately. Oliver would either think that Seth was joking, or that he was mental. He couldn't risk changing in front of Oliver, either. Once in wolf form, he wouldn't recognize his best friend. He would only look like a tasty meal and he wouldn't put Oliver in that position.

Seth decided on something. He decided that he would get himself arrested so that when he changed, somebody would see it, but he would be behind bars, unable to hurt anyone. Perhaps they would even catch it on camera. Then, they would either accept him, though he didn't think that was likely, or they would end him. He wasn't sure which one he preferred.

Seth gave some thought to how he would get arrested. He could hike his leg and pee on something, but that was crass - even for a werewolf. He thought some more, considering mugging an old lady, taking candy from a baby, and even stealing a baby. He didn't like any of those. Finally, it came to him. He'd take an unloaded weapon into a convenience store and pretend to rob the place. He didn't want to take any money or anything, but he figured it would get him thrown in a jail a while.

So, Seth grabbed a handgun, made sure it wasn't loaded and that he left all ammunition at home. He threw on a dark hoodie and found the nearest convenience store. He walked in and browsed the aisles, waiting for the store to be empty besides him and the cashier. Once the store was empty, he walked up to the counter with the gun and demanded that the cashier empty the till. The cashier remained calm, fortunately. Seth didn't want a real altercation.

When the cashier handed the money over, he asked for some of the items that were kept behind the counter. He was stalling for time, hoping the police would show up soon.

Seth kept making requests and the cashier continued to meet his demands. When the police failed to show up, Seth told the cashier not to bother and left everything there on the counter before exiting the store.

Seth needed to do something fast, or he was going to change and everyone would be in danger. He got in his car and headed for a lonely spot in the country. He decided he would lock his car doors, change in the car, and remain there until he changed back. He considered calling Oliver with very specific instructions. He was becoming desperate for someone, anyone, to know his secret, but he couldn't let anyone get hurt.

He called Oliver, told him where he was, and asked him to come out there. He told him not to get out of his own car for any reason. If Seth, or anything else, should escape from his car, Oliver was to keep his doors locked and drive away - fast.

Oliver thought that the request was incredibly odd, but Seth was his best friend, so he went with it. He drove out to the spot that Seth had given him directions to and sat in his car, watching Seth. Oliver was tempted to fall asleep, but kept his eyes open for Seth's sake.

As the moon came out from behind the clouds, Oliver saw something he never thought possible. Something he'd never forget for as long as he lived. He sat in his car watching his best friend change forms. Oliver said a few choice words, unable to peel his eyes away from the scene in front of him. Once the change had taken place, his friend was no longer there. Instead, it was a big, ravenous wolf.

The wolf had glowing yellow eyes that seemed dazed and confused for a moment. Once the wolf gained its mental footing, it looked around at the car it was in. The prison its human form had created for itself. And it was angry. It clawed at the windows and slashed at the seats in the car.

Oliver was frightened, but he remembered that Seth wanted him to see this. And he was pretty sure he knew why. If Seth had told him that he was a werewolf, Oliver would have laughed it off. Seeing it with his own eyes, he wasn't sure what to make of it.

Oliver spent the night keeping an eye on the wolf in Seth's car. It never got out, thankfully. He worked all night on what to say to his friend when he changed back. Once Seth changed back into his human form, he slumped over in the back seat, sound asleep - or knocked unconscious. Oliver wasn't sure which. When Seth came to, Oliver checked him over to make sure he was okay before pulling his best friend into a hug.

"I understand why you had to show me," Oliver told Seth. "It changes nothing, but we'll need to talk about this soon."

Seth nodded, grateful tears streaming down his cheeks. Finally, somebody knew his secret, and he was still loved and accepted in spite of it.

Trick or Treat

Her nails grew long as her skin shrunk tighter to her bones. The aging spell had worked and it would only last for a time. Helga cackled like the witch she'd become. It was Halloween night and she hoped the children would truly be spooked by her appearance. She'd considered entering the neighborhood costume contest, but decided that it wouldn't be fair.

She gazed into the mirror admiring her thin gray hair, long and wiry. Her nose had grown to a large hooked appendage on her face. Warts dotted her now ugly and wrinkled face, her smile filled with crooked, rotting teeth.

Helga cackled one more time before changing into her witching robe. Grabbing her cauldron full of candy treats she'd purchased from the grocery store, she sat by the front door, waiting for the children to come trick-or-treating in their costumes.

The first group of children came by and Helga was delighted. There was a witch among them, like herself, but she looked adorable. There was also a jack-o-lantern, a superhero, and a little devil. As soon as she'd opened the door, the children said, "Trick or treat!" Helga smiled, her sagging eyes bright with joy. She complimented the little tykes on their wonderful costumes, holding out her cauldron for them to select their candy. They each took a piece or two before saying, "Happy Halloween!" and walking away.

Helga loved Halloween, and not for the significance it held as a witch, but for the joy she received at seeing children dressed up. She looked back fondly at her childhood Halloween memories. She'd always been very creative with her costumes. She didn't know magic back then, so her costumes were all handmade and designed by herself.

One year, perhaps her favorite pre-magic costume, she dressed up as a popular, but also unpopular politician. The entire left side of her body was a bulldog with red lipstick. The other side was dressed professionally, and wore glasses. She received a lot of compliments on that particular costume. She figured it was probably because those that liked the politician thought it was an honor, while those who did not like the politician thought it was a clever mockery. Either way, it was her best pre-magic work.

When the evening was over, Helga looked at herself in the mirror. The aging spell should have been wearing off by now, but she remained the same. She decided to go watch an episode of her favorite hunting brothers while she waited for the spell to wear off. When the episode was finished, Helga looked at her hands and found that they had not changed at all.

Panicked, she ran to the bathroom to look in the mirror. She hadn't changed at all. It was like she was...stuck this way. Helga's heart began to pound and sweat began to bead on her wrinkly, wart-covered face. She couldn't stay like this. She started to feel faint and remembered that she was in an old woman's body now. She needed to stay calm before she died of heart attack or stroke.

Helga went through the spell in the book, looking for any indication that this could happen. She found nothing. She searched through all of her spell books, finding nothing useful. She called another witch, a friend who had taught her everything she knows about magic. The friend came over as quickly as she could.

"Helga! You look terrible," she could barely contain her laughter.

"Very funny, Mildred. I'm terrified!"

"You should be. This is not what our magic is for."

"I only do this once a year! It's never gone wrong like this." Helga was beginning to become frustrated that Mildred wasn't taking this more seriously.

"Looking at you, I can tell you what's happened," Mildred said, unsuccessfully hiding her smirk.

"You...what?! Is it serious? Will I be like this forever?" Mixed feelings overwhelmed Helga. She was hopeful that Mildred could help her, and scared that she could not.

"Another witch has played a trick on you, rather than receiving a treat," Mildred said. She had a look on her face that told Helga she'd been ridiculous for panicking.

Helga felt foolish. "A trick." she said, embarrassed.

Mildred nodded her head, more sympathetic now.

"It happens," Mildred explained, "but it usually happens to brand new witches. Not witches of your level."

Helga paced back and forth. Stopping suddenly, she asked, "How long before I can expect it to wear off?"

Mildred gave Helga another once-over. "It should wear off by the time you wake up in the morning.

With a sigh of relief, Helga hugged Mildred, thanking her for coming over and talking her through everything. Soon, Mildred left and Helga fixed herself a hot bath. Her bones were achy and she wanted to release the stress of the evening by soaking in some jetted bubbles before going to bed.

The next morning, Mildred hadn't heard from Helga, so she decided to pop by and make sure everything was ok. Helga didn't answer the door and she wasn't answering her phone, which Mildred could hear from inside the house when she called the number.

Beginning to really worry, Mildred pulled out the spare house key that Helga had given her and let herself in. She searched the living room first, then the kitchen. When she went to Helga's bedroom she found Helga lying there on the bed. She could have been sleeping peacefully, but she didn't see her chest rising or falling to indicate she was breathing.

Mildred checked her pulse and found nothing. She called 911 and they pronounced her Dead-on-Arrival. Her heart had failed. Her normal appearance was back, which means she must have died before the change.

Mildred felt terrible. She was the one who'd played the trick on Helga. And now, her best friend was dead.

Nevariel's Inheritance

Nevariel had lived two hundred long years with his parents. His father's abuse over those centuries was forever etched in Nevariel's otherwise perfect elven skin. Nevariel was waiting at the family table in his home. The Alder of Elders was on his way to deliver the news of Nevariel's parents' passing, and to announce the resulting inheritance. This wasn't news for the two-hundred-year-old elf because Nevariel was there when his father died.

His father was dead, and good riddance. Nevariel caught himself. It was both difficult and imperative that he portray an appropriate amount of grief and sorrow for the loss of his father. It was difficult because he saw this as the beginning of a new abuse and control free era; imperative because he was the one responsible for his father's demise and, if he were to be found out, he'd be exiled to the Madlands. This would seriously impede his end goal.

So, Nevariel sat at the table, intentionally and skillfully looking anxious about the arrival of the Alder. He fidgeted under the watchful eyes of the Guardian elves. Their presence was not intimidating to Nevariel, nor was it meant to be. With his father's murderer on the loose and as the only living heir to his title, he was to be under very close watch to ensure his safety.

His father had been a part of the Council of Elders in the Spiritwood Forest. He was a brute on the Council, but they never saw anything like the wrath Nevariel experienced at home. He could often see pity in the eyes of some of the Elders who suspected his father's cruelty at home. He despised their pity. It was a part of the driving force that caused Nevariel to end his father's life.

Finally, the Alder arrived. Surrounded by his own Guardian elves, he entered with all of the authority of one befitting his title. Yet, a quiet wisdom emanated from his very old, but very strong body. Though still unafraid, and rather beaming internally with joy, Nevariel looked stricken when he received the news. He wore shock like a mask so cleverly designed that he very nearly fooled himself.

He forced a tear from his eyes, mimicking sadness as he allowed his shoulders to sag and looked towards the floor with a blank stare. He was an excellent actor thanks to years of practice around a father who could become violent at any moment; particularly when Nevariel showed any sort of emotional weakness.

The Alder spoke again, his deep, kind voice rumbling, "Nevariel, this means that you will take your father's place on the Council of the Elders."

Nevariel shifted, pretending to be uncomfortable with the news.

"Son, it means that you will carry on your father's legacy."

Nevariel winced at that. He didn't want to carry on his father's legacy. He intended to blaze his own trail through The Callows. He nearly scolded himself internally for the wince, but decided it could easily be portrayed as a sting of acceptance that his father was really, truly, sadly gone. This would do.

The Alder patted Nevariel on the shoulder as they made eye contact. The Alder seemed to know something and it was showing in his eyes. Nevariel maintained eye contact as the Alder continued to search the depths beyond the pupils.

The Alder's face betrayed a glimpse of disappointment before smiling with kindness at Nevariel. "It's not too late," The Alder whispered in Nevariel's ear.

This caused Nevariel to go rigid. The Alder was often cryptic, but this was a new level. Before Nevariel could ask him what he meant, The Alder was out the door and his guards with him. Nevariel was tempted to sit there and stew over what The Alder could have meant, but he'd learned long ago that it was better to just ask directly, or let it go entirely. He chose the latter and retreated to his bedroom.

He had inherited this house from his parents. Though he loved his mother, the memories of his interactions with his father seemed etched into everything. He was going to change everything; his home, his path, his future. Nevariel's smile spread from one pointed ear to the other. He would have it all.

Sarra's Wedding

Sarra loved a good wedding, Elven or human. They were always a beautiful celebration of the union of two souls destined for one another. The beauty of the decorations, the dancing and laughter - every last moment and detail so beautifully planned and spontaneous at the same time.

She supposed she would enjoy a dragon wedding as well, though she'd never been invited to one. Sarra felt different about this wedding, however. She didn't get to plan it the way she'd wanted. She was permitted to choose some things, like her dress and the flowers, but so many of the other details were planned for her - including her groom.

She'd dreamed about her wedding since she was a little girl. Sarra had imagined her Elven community joined by her human friends gathered under the blossoming trees to celebrate a joyous union of the deepest love and commitment. This wasn't exactly the case for her.

Sarra was about to walk down the aisle to wed King Federick in front of his entire kingdom. Nerves shot through her like bolts of bright lightning, her internal sobs like thunder in her ears. She was entirely unconscious of her dress. Being the Queen-to-Be meant that she had several servant girls making sure her dress was always adjusted properly.

The crowd that had showed up to her wedding was large, much larger than she had ever conceived probable. Her parents were there, somewhere in the crowd, but otherwise, she didn't know a soul.

Sarra tried not to notice the crowd that gawked at her, whispering to one another. They seemed to appreciate the beautifully fitted lace and satin on her dress. It billowed out into a ballroom style bubble around her hips and had a long, flowing train trailing behind her.

Children tossed her favorite flowers, dragon flowers, before her as she made her way down the aisle. The fiery orange, red, and white flowers made a soft cushion to walk on. She had to remind herself to breathe, smile, and not clench her bouquet too harshly.

Truth be told, she felt a little ridiculous. She wasn't royalty. She wasn't even technically nobility. Not being human meant she wasn't born with a title in the human community. Federick didn't know she wasn't human, and it was imperative that he and the entirety of his kingdom remain ignorant of this fact. Humans were unaware of the elves who went to great lengths to maintain their secrecy.

Sarra was chosen by the Elven Elders to marry the King, though she did not know him. She'd met him once, the day he selected her to be his bride. It was awkward for both of them, but it was a fleeting moment that held little value in Sarra's heart. She'd wanted to marry for love, but since she'd been selected by the Elders to marry Federick, she knew he would select her to be his bride. The Elders had used magic to make sure of it.

She made it down the aisle and took her place beside Federick. He was behaving a little less Kingly than she expected, his boyish grin stretching across his handsome face from one ear to the other. She relaxed a little knowing he wasn't being so formal and uptight as she expected.

She accepted his hand and he led her up the stairs to stand directly before the thrones. He gently turned her to face him. When she looked into his emerald eyes, she saw magic. Not the magic that the Elders had used to secure her position, but a pure magic that came from within Federick. It was love, adoration, and complete joy. Her heart fell into his in that moment, and it was the beginning of the fairytale she'd never dreamed possible.

It wasn't long before Sarra became pregnant. She was worried for the child, the one she knew would be a girl, thanks to the Foretelling. Federick was ecstatic at the news that his bride was pregnant. He had great plans for the child that he was certain would be a boy. In the end, Sarra was right. She'd given birth to a beautiful baby girl. They named her Alys.

Sarra never became pregnant again, much to Federick's disappointment. Though Sarra never forgot about the Foretelling, and what it would mean for her daughter, it soon became easier and easier to think that maybe it wouldn't happen. Maybe Alys would just get to live a regular life. Well, regular for royalty. Maybe Alys wouldn't have to face off with the dragons after all.

Tobias' Sacrifice

Tobias' heart twisted in horror at the sight of Alys being held at knifepoint by Nigha. To someone who didn't know Alys, she wouldn't appear afraid. Tobias, however, knew her better than anybody. She was the other half of his soul.

He couldn't watch and he couldn't look away. Though the Elder was only showing him a vision of a possibility, it still stole the breath from his lungs. He would die for Alys, though he certainly hoped he wouldn't have to.

The Elder circled him slowly, soaking up Tobias' fear like it was his source of daily nutrients. Tobias was willing to do anything, *anything* to keep Alys safe and alive. It was proving to be a very difficult task, but the Elder said he had something to offer. He didn't trust the Elder, but Tobias was growing desperate.

"You want to keep Alys safe, yes?" the Elder asked. His voice was higher in pitch than most men.

It gave Tobias the feeling one might get when hearing a dragon's claws scrape across lava rock. It grated on Tobias' nerves.

"Of course. That's all I want."

"But, it's not *all* you want, is it, boy?" the Elder drawled.

Tobias did want more. Yes, he wanted Alys safe, but in addition, he wanted Alys. He wanted her heart. He wanted her to love him and want him the way he loved and wanted her.

The Elder nodded. "Yes...I see that desire in your heart. Who can blame you? She *is* lovely."

Tobias cringed inwardly. The idea of the Elder noticing Alys' loveliness left him with a sick feeling.

The Elder stopped circling, pausing as if to think. "I have a proposition for you," the Elder stated. He did not lift his head to look at Tobias. He only lifted his steely gray eyes. The Elder proceeded as though he were proceeding with caution.

Tobias barely noticed.

"I can help you keep Alys safe, but I can also give you the deeper desire embedded in your heart."

Tobias looked at the Elder in wonder. Could he really have it all? "What will it cost me?" Tobias asked. He was leery of the Elder. He knew nothing about him and now he was offering Tobias everything he ever wanted. If being adopted has taught him anything, it's that nothing is ever free.

"You are very perceptive," the Elder said. "What I require in exchange for Alys' safety and love is the necklace you secretly wear about your neck."

Tobias instinctively reached up to touch the gem that lay hidden beneath his shirt. It was the only piece of his parents that he had left. He doesn't remember them, but that necklace was the only thing they'd given him. It was his only connection to a past that still held so many unanswered questions.

"How do I know that you'll come through on your end of the bargain?" Tobias asked. He'd already decided it was worth giving up the gem for, though it left him feeling numb.

The Elder could see the resignation in Tobias' eyes. He felt victorious, and did little to hide it. "Magic will bind us, child. Hand the necklace to me and you will find things quite changed when you return to your lovely Alys."

Tobias held onto the gem of the necklace a moment, as though saying his goodbyes. Then, with stiff resolution, Tobias yanked the necklace from his neck, walked to the Elder, and deposited the neckless into the Elder's hands. Tobias' breathing was uneven. Tears threatened to escape from his eyes. He swallowed hard.

"You have made a wise choice, my boy," the Elder said, not taking his eyes off of the necklace. "You may leave."

Tobias nodded curtly and walked out of the cave. Hope mixed with fear and guilt in his heart. Hope that he would have Alys, fear that he just gave up his dearest possession and that it still wouldn't work, guilt at magicking Alys into loving him the way he loved her.

Hope again, because he just gave the last part of himself in order to get what he so desperately wanted.

The King's Discovery

Federick wasn't on the battlefield, but observing from a vantage point. He could see it. His victory was on the horizon. The dragons were beginning to fall back in defeat, his military encouraged and strengthened by this knowledge. He looked out on the battlefield watching the different battles, and that's when he spotted her.

Panic grabbed his heart and squeezed tight. Alys was on the battlefield. To make things worse, she wasn't wearing her battle garb. She was on the battlefield completely unprotected. A particular movement caught his eye. Odin, the great dragon lord of the black horde was making his way toward Alys. No. No. He couldn't allow it. Odin's horde had already taken the most precious person in his life. He would not allow him to take another.

As Odin approached Alys, Federick saw nothing else. He made his way toward them, dodging swords and staffs. He stopped cold when he saw Odin crouch to the ground in a rage, reaching for his dragon fire. He didn't have time to stand still and watch. He continued making his way toward them. He saw Alys kneel and caress Odin's cheek. Federick burned with rage. When had she become so familiar with the dragon lord?

Odin stood and held Alys' face in his hands. He said something to her before turning and walking away. Odin called for his horde to retreat. Federick stopped again, disbelief and rage coloring his vision. He was close to wiping dragons from existence, and Alys sent them away with a caress?!

Finally, he made it to Alys. He grabbed her by the arms, shaking her. "What have you done?" he screamed at her. "What. Have. You. Done?" he seethed.

Alys remained calm, which enraged him all the more.

"I told you, Father. There can be peace. We don't have to kill them," Alys replied.

Federick was torn. He was certain he didn't want "peace" with the dragons, but how could he make Alys see that Odin and his horde were a danger to all? He released Alys' arms and began to pace.

"How long have you been familiar with Odin?" Federick asked with disdain.

"I don't see how that matters, Father. I see something in him that you refuse to acknowledge. Maybe if you would let go of your anger long enough, you could see it too."

Why did Alys insist on causing him pain and rage? He considered disowning her, but who would be left to take the throne once he was gone from this world? His hatred for dragons boiled in his blood. He would see them all suffer and die for what happened to Sarra.

"If you are not with me, Alys, you have become my enemy, and an enemy of the kingdom. You should hope to never see me again because if you do, it will be the last time you see anything in this life," Federick declared with a solid resolution in his mind.

He turned from her and walked away across the now empty battlefield and back to his vantage point. A new fuel was added to his hate-fire that he kept aflame for the dragons. Odin turned his daughter against him, and he would pay the most. Federick would guarantee it.

Odin's Prickly Memories

Alys had flowing auburn hair that pricked at memories long buried beneath his new purpose. Forgetting was Odin's golden rule because remembering...remembering was just unacceptable. He scoffed. Dancing with humans was unacceptable, but the girl moved with a graceful strength that threatened the exhumation of his darkest memory.

She seemed to notice the flicker of fear in his smoky eyes, and met them with a studious contemplation in her own. He hastily built a wall behind his eyes, not wanting her to see any more than she already had. Her emerald gaze was penetrating, placing his freshly erected wall in danger of being crushed beneath her stare.

His draconian heart began to race. Fear tangled with longing snaked around his chest, constricting him till he couldn't catch his breath. Humans were daft, disgusting creatures, and yet, this one seemed to see right through him. No, not through him, *into* him. She couldn't possibly know the details of his pain or his loss, but somehow, she knew that the pain and loss was there, buried deep beneath the dark soil of his soul.

He needed to leave, desperately. The dance wasn't over, but he couldn't live another second beneath the stare of this dangerous, beautiful, horrible human girl. He stopped dancing and left as quickly as possible, Alys' knowing stare following him out of the dance hall.

Acknowledgments

To my husband and my girls who read my stories, whether they want to or not, because they support me in my endeavors.

To Rae and Tiff who always have my back and remind me frequently that I can do this author thing. The love, support, and safe space to share *everything* has been one of the greatest blessings of my life.

To Liza Kane, who provided many of the prompts for the stories I've written and compiled in this volume. If you're a creative (writer, crafter, artist, etc.), check her group out on Facebook: The Thriving Artist Collective. You won't be disappointed.

To Debbie Burns, who helped me reclaim my dream of doing what I love, and making money at it. I'm eternally grateful for the support and the atmosphere that you have created in Creative Central Fictionpreneurs. If you're a female writer, her group on Facebook is a **must**.

To my brother, the best Wookiee, for his help, support, and encouragement.

Last, but not least, I want to thank my readers. Without you, I would lack so much of the fulfillment I receive from writing. Thank you!

Made in the USA
Middletown, DE
26 February 2018